THE BLUE HOUSE

Nigel Parsons

The Blue House is a work of fiction. All the characters are fictitious, and any resemblance to any real person, living or dead, is entirely coincidental.

By the same author:

Manouche: Living with the Gypsies of France

A personal account of the author's years spent living with a nomadic group of Manouche Gypsies in the 1970s, and his search to find them again in the present day.

Three Lives

The lives of three families become unexpectedly intertwined, but one is intent on the destruction of what they perceive as an unjust and immoral society. This book takes the reader through the major events of the second half of the twentieth century and the first part of the twenty-first which shaped the world we live in, as seen through the eyes of the protagonists, into a dystopian near future until its tragic and shocking denouement.

This one is for Daniel & Simon, sons and best friends. #Lads.

Their mother, Monica.

And not forgetting Brandy, my constant (four-legged) companion.

PROLOGUE

The Present

The view outside is disappointing. The house is a few miles outside Zürich and seems to be on some kind of minor industrial estate. I had hoped to see distant mountains maybe, even a glimpse of snow, but instead out of one window all I can see is a large grey storage shed, and out of the other a stretch of wasteland covered in wild yellow flowers and a pond overgrown with weeds.

The room itself is nice enough, though, wood-panelled in the Swiss way, a jug of water on the bedside table, and some flowers – I think they're lilies, but flowers aren't my strong point – on the chest of drawers.

Being Switzerland, it's also spotlessly clean, and there's a huge flat-screen television on the wall, plus, of course, an ensuite bathroom, which is what you'd expect for the kind of money they are charging. It *is* very expensive, but then I suppose you could call it a once-in-a-lifetime experience, so worth every penny.

Outside the door I can hear occasional soft murmurings and the wheeling of various trolleys. I'm waiting for my room service dinner; I have ordered steak tartare with a rocket side salad, and strawberries with cream for dessert. I might also order a glass of local pinot noir to wash it down, although I rarely drink these days. In truth I'm not very hungry either; it's been a long time since I had that ravenous feeling when your stomach is growling and your nostrils twitch at the aromas of approaching food. I miss such simple pleasures.

Finally, there's a discreet knock on the door, and a lovely, smiley girl with blond plaited hair wheels in my dinner. At first, I wonder if she's an apparition, but she's not. She sets the overbed table and carefully adjusts its height, then lays it with a freshly starched tablecloth and napkin before putting down the cutlery, and finally the food. Her badge says she is called *A Nagy*, so I deduce there must be a Hungarian link, and she smells as fresh as the tablecloth. I wonder what the 'A' stands for, and I want to eat her rather than the food, but instead politely ask for my glass of pinot noir, which she dutifully goes to collect.

When she returns, I ask if she would mind sitting with me while I eat, telling her that 'to eat alone is to die alone'. She gives me one of her beautiful smiles and tells me of course not, and pulls up a chair. I ask about her name and whether she is Hungarian, and she says her parents fled the country after the 1956 revolution which was savagely put down by the Soviets. 'So ethnically I am Hungarian, but I suppose I am Swiss now.' She shrugs.

'So, what does the "A" stand for?'

'Alexandra, but you can call me Alex.'

We chat about this and that, about my life's exploits here, there and all over the place, and she listens attentively until I have finished eating and drained the last of the wine, then she clears the dishes and quietly leaves the room.

Replete, with the debris of my dinner cleared away, and left to myself again, I switch on the television and watch a game show which I don't understand; my German is quite good, but not good enough to unscramble the Swiss version of it. Outside, the sky is darkening, so I shuffle to the bathroom to relieve myself and clean my teeth without really understanding why I bother, and get back into bed.

I don't really want to go to sleep too quickly; tonight is too important, and I don't want to miss any of it. I think back on all the major events in my life, a life of travel and adventure and trying to understand the point of it all. I remember the women I have loved – Conceição in Brazil, Mercedes the Colombian, Polish Catherine in Nigeria, and most of all Iseult the Briton. I conjure up all of their images and wonder where they are now, but am happy to think I will soon be with Iseult again. And I also think of Roberto, who has become like a brother to me, and the adventures we shared. They were special times, and I would happily live them again.

Eventually, though, and too soon, my mind tires and my eyelids flutter shut and I drift off into a deep sleep, a smile on my face.

CHAPTER ONE

Mato Grosso, Brazil, 1978

The journey was about to get worse, much worse. What Tony was on the brink of discovering was that, whatever else Cuiabá's dubious claim to fame might be, it also marked the point where the asphalt road ended and became a red dust dirt track.

He was tall, just over six feet, and lean, twenty-seven years old, with close-cropped straw coloured hair, a prominent Adam's apple, startlingly deep blue eyes flecked with white, and an astonishingly deep voice which always commanded attention. It was not long before midnight, and he climbed wearily off the bus he had boarded in São Paulo, the country's grotesque money-making hub in the south, twenty-eight hours earlier.

It was mid-November, and he'd come to Brazil to escape the debris of a failed marriage and the grim winter weather in England; luckily there had been no children, and he'd been told that Brazil was a land of opportunity ideal for a fresh start. Specifically, he was heading to the Amazon rainforest, and on his giant map of South America had circled a name that looked about as far inland on the continent as you could get without starting to come out again on the other side. It was a frontier settlement called Porto Velho in the federal territory of Rondônia, still too young for the status of a state, some 1,500 miles northwest of São Paulo by air, or around 2,000 miles by road, and within striking distance of Brazil's border with Bolivia.

He'd spent two days in São Paulo, in a shabby room which formed part of a dingy boarding house off one of the main thoroughfares, where the transvestite proprietor had informed him that the city boasted a million prostitutes. It was the ugliest city he'd ever seen, a mix of multimillionaire mansions, with manicured lawns and white-gloved servants, surrounded by abject 'favelas': shanty towns without drainage or running water, overflowing with human misery. The yellow smog meant he rarely ventured out except to find something to eat, and when he did, it was with a damp handkerchief to cover his face, protection against the burning exhaust fumes.

On the second day, sitting in a food bar with a plate of *beefy* in front of him – some stringy, slightly undercooked meat, probably from one of Brazil's humpbacked zebu cows, with rice and beans – the man next to him asked what a gringo was doing there.

'I'm not a gringo, I'm English,' Tony told him, which elicited a shrug which seemed to suggest there was no difference. 'But I'm heading to Amazonia. I heard there were opportunities there.'

His companion, a thick-set man with bushy black hair greased back and eyebrows that met in the middle like a caterpillar, separating his forehead from the rest of his face, registered faint surprise for a second, then opened his mouth and gave forth a resounding 'Ha! Haa!' For a moment Tony thought he was about to choke, but then his face took on a solemn expression and he said, 'O Amazonia! O meo floresta muito bonito! My beautiful jungle! You really want to go there? Because me,' and he slapped his chest, 'I lived there for many years before.'

'You did? And?'

The man held out a plump, glistening hand to shake Tony's. 'Ernesto,' he announced.

'Tony.'

'Well, Mr Tony, listen to me, I give you some advice: maybe you should forget Amazonia.'

Tony wiped grease from his hand onto a paper napkin, and tried to speak through another morsel of the meat. 'Well, I've come this far, so no turning back now. Why don't you think I should go?'

Ernesto finished his food and cleaned his plate with a piece of bread, then leaned forwards and spoke through his thick moustache, which still had bits of rice sticking to it. 'Hey, listen,

Inglês, don't be angry. You know sometimes the Amazon is a beautiful place, but it is a wild place too, and if you go there, you will learn what nothing means.'

'What do you mean?' Tony pushed the remains of his food away and took a large slug of his Brahma Chopp beer.

'I mean you can fly there for days, up and down, without seeing nothing of nothing, only trees and water. Nothing is nothing, it's really nothing! Time doesn't exist there, nobody counts the time, what for? And when it rains, my friend, it really rains. It's non-stop for four, maybe five months, even longer sometimes, day and night, you can't move, it doesn't make any sense to move! You just wait. When you are there and it rains, the world doesn't exist anymore. And it's hot, so hot, it's a green hell. Instead of fire you get water, but still, it's a hell.'

Tony rummaged in his pocket for his packet of 'Hollywood Filtro' cigarettes and lit one, watching the blue smoke drift lazily upwards and then disperse as it came within range of the slowly churning ceiling fan. 'How long were you there?' he asked.

Ernesto shrugged again. 'More than three years. I had a dream to buy a farm. I was making a lot of money selling land for Citibank, for Mitsubishi, for other big companies.' He rubbed his thumb against two fingers as if feeling the banknotes. 'But when I finally had enough, I was attacked and everything was stolen. There are many bad people up there; you must be careful. So, in the end, I gave up and came back here. Now I drive a taxi.'

'Sorry to hear that,' Tony said. 'Will you go back?'

'Maybe. I don't know. I have children now, and Amazonia is hard for children.'

'I'm going to a place called Porto Velho. Do you know it?'

'Sure, I know it.' Ernesto chuckled, and the last bits of food fell from his moustache. 'I was in Rio Branco in Acre state, not so far from Rondônia. You have to be a macaco, a monkey, to live there. Civilisation, it doesn't exist there, there is no culture, there's no one to talk to, and maybe someone shoots you just because they don't like the colour of your eyes, or you can get a disease like malaria –

so many flies and mosquitos, bigger than you ever saw before! But it can be beautiful too.'

Selling land for the likes of Citibank and Mitsubishi somehow didn't fit with Tony's idea of a new Wild West brimming with opportunity, and he wondered what the multinationals were up to in the jungle. Instead of pursuing that, he asked, 'What about Indians? Did you see many of them?'

Again, Ernesto chuckled. 'Indios? I think you read the newspaper too much, my friend. I say if you travel in Amazonia, you can travel for years and not see a single Indio. I say it's easier to find and kill a puma than to find an Indio!'

'But lots of money, huh?'

'Yes, it's possible to get money very quickly in Amazonia, but truly it's for the next generation.'

'How do you mean?'

'For my children, or their children, because I tell you one thing, my friend,' and Ernesto assumed an earnest expression, his eyes gleaming as if with some secret yearning. 'Amazonia will mean a lot for the world one day. It is the future.'

'You really think so?'

'Oh, yes, Amazonia is a big reservoir for the world. One day it will feed much of the world. The world is going to fight a lot for food, and so Amazonia will be a source of peace. It will be a source of minerals, cattle, maybe cotton, soybeans. It's a big insurance for the whole world, and we will conquer it, don't think it's not true.'

It didn't sound much like becoming a source for peace to Tony, especially with the multinationals involved. To him it sounded more like a source of future conflict, but he didn't say so, given that Ernesto was still in full flow.

'And you know, there is only one way to colonise Amazonia, and that is to invade it! Yes! People are dying there, much money is being swallowed and many illusions destroyed, but we will win! And this is how it must be! I believe it!' With that, Ernesto slid off his stool and held out his meaty hand to Tony again. 'Now, my friend, I must go, I must make money, but I wish you luck.'

'Thank you; it sounds as if I might need it.'

Tony watched him lumber out of the bar, finished his cigarette, then followed.

The next day he boarded the overnight bus to Cuiabá, deep in Mato Grosso: the first stage of his journey to Amazonia. He could have flown, but he needed to conserve his funds, and the bus was by far the cheapest option. And it wasn't too bad, a luxury model with reclining seats, tinted windows, air conditioning, and even a toilet at the back. Tony slung his soft leather carry bag into the overhead luggage rack, then eased back his seat, placed his straw hat over his face, and dozed off as the bus pulled out of the station.

Dawn found them wedged in a four-hour hold-up caused by a spectacular accident in the Brazilian fashion. They waited for the mangled wreckage of half a dozen VW Beetles and an ancient truck which had been carrying watermelons to be shoved to one side, for the watermelons to be recaptured and the bodies to be carried away, then sped on past a fading green landscape which rapidly turned into a pale savannah.

Soon all evidence of the grass disappeared and the earth boiled. The land was scorched red, with only a few tufts of spiky vegetation clinging to life through roots reaching deep down, and skeletal, misshapen trees, stunted from birth. Wayside settlements became more and more sparse until there were none any more, just mile after mile of nothing sweltering under the brilliant glare until dusk brought relief.

When they pulled into a slumbering Cuiabá a couple of hours before midnight, only the bus station was still awake. Tony stretched his aching limbs, then established that there was an ongoing bus for Porto Velho at noon the next day. There seemed no point in lingering in Cuiabá. He paid the equivalent of a couple of pounds for a bed in a barren room painted orange and blue in a nearby hostel and, after spraying himself with copious amounts of repellent against the blood-sucking mosquitos, fell into a fitful sleep.

CHAPTER TWO

INTO THE AMAZON

Tony awoke early and breakfasted in the still cool shade of the street on thick sweet Brazilian coffee and goiabada jam, made from red guavas and sugar, from a tin.

While he was at it, he was thrilled by the sight of his first cowboy. There for all the world to see was this skinny, weatherbeaten old man with hide riding boots complete with tinkling spurs, even if the star on his black felt hat was a white plastic stick-on. And he was on a bicycle rather than a horse, pedalling lethargically by on an old bone-shaker. It was hardly John Wayne, but still!

Tony swilled back the last of his coffee, jammed his hat on his head, picked up his bag, and crossed the dusty road back to the bus station, where the clerk gave him a mischievous smirk when he asked for a ticket to Porto Velho.

'Porto Velho – muito horas! Many, many hours, and the estrada, the road, it's bad, very bad.'

Ignoring the warning, Tony paid for his ticket and joined a gaggle of migrating peasants to squeeze onto an obsolete machine reminiscent of the school buses he'd dutifully ridden twenty years previously, barely forcing his long legs in between the seats made for children half his height. There was no sign of air conditioning or reclining seats this time.

After a short delay, while the other passengers argued amongst themselves seemingly about anything and everything, the driver finally crossed himself, muttered three Hail Marys, and they moved off. The old bus shook and rattled on the gravel and dirt track – Tony felt that to call it a 'road' would be a bit of an exaggeration –

and red dust blew in through the open windows, covering everything with a thin film. An hour and a half later, they broke down.

Surviving the next forty-plus hours soon developed into a grim matter of *'don't count the minutes'* and *'turn the mind off, we'll soon be there'* determination, interspersed with occasional welcome slumbers from which Tony usually awoke with a jolt and a sore neck as the bus ground to a halt once more, breaking down yet again. Progress was painstakingly slow, but every time the old beast wheezed to a halt, the driver somehow managed to cajole it back into life, sometimes with the help of a spanner, or with a hammer and a few kicks, and some colourful language. At four in the morning, though, he managed to drive into a patch of soft sand and eased off the accelerator, before realising his mistake and revving wildly again until the rear wheels were buried up to the chassis.

Everyone gathered outside to examine the problem, and after much discussion and handwaving a vain effort was made to push the vehicle forwards while the driver revved the engine some more. Tony rubbed the sleep from his eyes and cast around for a flat piece of wood, which he used to begin digging at the hidden wheels. The driver and his mate joined in, scraping away at the other side of the bus, until their backs ached and their knuckles were rubbed raw, and they were all covered in a thick coat of red dust. Then they placed crude ramps in front of the tyres, and they were ready to give it a try when Tony realised that the three of them were alone out there under the stars. The bus was suspiciously quiet, and a gentle chorus of snores drifted out into the moonlight.

'For fuck's sake!' Tony swore.

The driver looked in through the door, then turned and gave a shrug. 'Amanhã, tomorrow,' he said. They weren't going anywhere until it was daylight.

Luckily a passing truck stopped a couple of hours later and dragged them back on to the track, and soon they were off again.

The bleak desert landscape stayed with them well into the second day. The heat was soporific, the air suffocating, the choking dust blocking the nose and congealing in the ears. Tony felt himself bouncing and jolting for hours on end, until his whole body was in torment and his head throbbed with a dull pain. The only brief respites came when they stopped at occasional clusters of ragged adobe huts where they could relieve themselves and buy some lukewarm coffee or a soft drink. Filthy children squatted on pots in full view and mangy dogs roamed about searching for scraps. There seemed to be no reason for these clusters of huts to be there at all; nothing could be grown, but probably the road itself was the reason, providing the only source of income.

By evening, though, some vegetation began to stage a gradual comeback. To begin with it was just a sporadic tree here and there, but then it slowly became greener and more dense and finally even lush as they passed into Rondônia. All of the passengers looked out of the windows expectantly for their first sight of the world's largest and most dreadful rainforest, but they were greeted instead by a strong smell of burning and were suddenly surrounded by thick smoke which hid the jungle from view and blocked out the sinking sun.

It was the dry season, and Amazonia's new settlers were busy driving the foliage relentlessly back, by tractor, by machete, and by fire. It was in the 1970s that the mass deforestation of the Amazon, an area the size of India which spans nine countries and comprises half of the world's rainforests, really went into overdrive. What Tony didn't know then was that within fifty years some twenty percent of the forest would be destroyed, to the point that it would risk collapsing in on itself and transitioning to scrubby savannah.

They made a short stop in Vilhena, a one-horse town of rubber tappers and smallholdings, and then they were able to start counting off the last few hundred miles to Porto Velho. Where they could see it through gaps in the smoke, the jungle had been cleared back from either side of the dirt road for several hundred yards, leaving a stubby grass strip where scrawny zebu cattle eked out an existence between the blackened and slashed roots and plants. Soon enough they began to meet the huge yellow earth movers and bulldozers of the army, the advance parties of the road-laying machines, and then miraculously they were on tarmac again, driving past outlying shacks that heralded the beginnings of Porto Velho itself.

Tony unwound himself from his seat, offered up a prayer of thanks for having survived the journey, then clambered out with his bag and stretched his aching limbs to get some circulation back in them.

A cluster of vaqueiros – local cowboys – lazing in the shade of the bus station looked up with interest at the sweat-stained, dirt-covered gringo. They took him in slowly, digesting the information of his presence through pondering eyes. Tony was an object of curiosity for them likely to far exceed anything else that had happened that week – since, probably, the local diamond prospectors had last come into town for their one weekend in six out of the jungle and ended up shooting a taverna full of holes during a drunken orgy that raged unabated from Friday night through to Monday morning.

As Tony made to move off and explore the town, two of the vaqueiros slid off their backsides, adjusted their belts and holsters, which didn't quite fit their Japanese replicas of German revolvers, and followed him at a respectable distance. Tony was aware of the tail but took little notice of his followers as he made his way through a maze of dusty streets, down to the port on the Madeira River, a major tributary of the Amazon itself. It would have been impossible to imagine that in time this ramshackle place of shanty towns would be home to more than half a million people, driven by cassiterite mining and intensive cattle farming.

Between the lean-tos and hastily thrown up shacks, Tony wrinkled his nose at the stench of the open drainage and breathed negligence in the air, but there was something else too, something that could only be described as the 'spirit' of Amazonia, the pioneer spirit which seemed to permeate everything; this was a frontier.

He turned back and eventually arrived at the main square and the town's principal street, a two-laned and flagpole-lined affair some two hundred yards long, with yawning pot holes. It boasted the grandiose title of Avenida Presidente Dutra in honour of some long-forgotten dictator.

Tony's posse of cowboys stopped at the corner of the square and watched as he approached what seemed to be the only sign of life, a café called Califa. All the other shops and offices seemed to be shuttered up against the heat. Inside, Tony made the futile gesture of wiping sweat from his brow, pulled up a stool at the bar while dropping his bag on the floor, and ordered a bottle of exorbitant but welcome ice-cold Brahma Chopp beer.

CHAPTER THREE

Roberto

The level of Tony's second bottle was ominously close to the bottom, and he was beginning to feel light-headed, when the still of the afternoon was shattered by the tortured screech of tyres burning rubber on the avenida outside. Tony turned on his stool to see a dust-covered bright red Ford utility truck come to a halt outside, from which stepped a man in a skimpy white T-shirt and jeans.

The man moved with an agility that defied his huge forearms and square shoulders, and had a strong, angular face with a firm jaw, a jutting forehead and black ringlets. He looked a similar age to Tony, or maybe a couple of years older. He strode into the Califa, followed by a monstrous black hound with a drooling red tongue, and took a barstool one along from Tony, who regarded him with interest.

A glass of fresh orange juice was set before the newcomer, and he drained half of it in one thirst-quenching gulp. Then, aware of Tony's gaze, he swivelled to return it.

'Bom dia,' he said.

'Afraid I don't really speak Portuguese, não falo Português... Inglês?' Tony answered.

'English? Really? What are you doing here?'

'You speak English?'

'I try, but there is little chance here. See for yourself, these people, they are estúpido!'

The bar was empty apart from them and an olive-skinned mulatta girl busy slicing an avocado for a health-giving vitamina drink. A trio of fans hung from the ceiling, spinning lazily, churning the thick air, while flies crawled with impunity on every surface, eager to try their luck on some greasy cold fritters stored in a grimy glass showcase.

'So, do you have a name?' the man asked.

'Tony. I've just got here off the bus – all the way from São Paulo.'

'Wow, that's crazy! You took the bus all that way? We have airplanes, you know. I'm Roberto, by the way. So, tell me, why did you do that? And why are you here? I'm intrigued.' He signalled for the girl to bring two more beers.

Tony smiled and shrugged. He couldn't really explain it, and in any case was starting to have second thoughts. 'Yeah, it was a terrible journey, don't think I'd do it again, and to be honest not sure why I did in the first place. Maybe to see the country? And flying was quite expensive. As for what I'm doing here, well, I needed to get away from London, and I heard there were opportunities up here. But maybe it was a stupid idea now that I think about it, and from what I've seen of Porto Velho.'

Roberto nodded and sipped at his beer. 'Maybe, maybe not,' he said reflectively. 'Yes, there are opportunities, but nothing is easy up here. What do you plan to do, though, now that you are here? You know we call it the arse of Brazil?'

'I didn't,' Tony said, with a laugh. 'But first I guess find somewhere to stay, then have a look around. If nothing comes up, then I'll probably just have to retrace my steps.'

Roberto nodded again. He was enjoying the encounter, the chance to speak with someone from the outside world. 'Look, how about this?' he said suddenly, making up his mind. 'Why don't you come back with me? I have a farm here; well, I am *making* a farm, not far out of town. Now I have only a few cows, chickens, some fruit, that kind of thing. But I could use some help, and some company. I can't afford to pay you, but you will have somewhere to stay, and food. It will give you time to think about things.'

'Are you serious?'

'Sure, I'm serious. It's not very comfortable, but it's something.

Maybe you'd like to think about it?'

'I've thought about it!' Tony exclaimed. 'And the answer is yes! That's really kind; someone up there is looking after me.' He pointed to the ceiling. 'And, anyway, what have I got to lose? If it doesn't work out, then there's always Plan B.'

'Plan B?'

'Actually, there isn't one, but I'll cross that bridge when I come to it.'

Roberto grinned. 'Good, then it is decided. Take your bag and let's go.' He shouted for the bill, startling the girl. 'You have to shout here,' he said to Tony, 'otherwise they don't hear, just dream all the time.'

Outside, the heat hit Tony like a brick wall and he immediately starting sweating profusely. He went to put his bag in the back of the truck, but Roberto stopped him. 'Better to keep it in the cabin. Otherwise, if we stop, someone can take it. You have to be careful with everything here.'

The huge dog, which had followed them out of the Califa, jumped into the back as Roberto dropped the tailgate. 'His name is Senice,' Roberto said, 'but don't be afraid; he is big, but just a baby still.'

'A great Dane?'

'Yes, I bought him in São Paulo, cost a lot of money!'

CHAPTER FOUR

THE WATERFALL

Tony was Brahma Chopp lightheaded and spoke little as they sped out of Porto Velho, past neon-lit stores with products from abroad next to brightly coloured stalls selling everything from exotic fruits to T-shirts, hammocks and sarongs. Most of the streets seemed to have been torn up for repairs or were falling apart quicker than they were being built, mangy dogs rolled in the dust, and the miserable huts of imported labourers huddled together on the ill-defined outskirts of the town. Soon they were back on the red scar of the highway that stretched all the way back to Cuiabá, and were once again enveloped in smoke.

'All the time burning!' Roberto shouted above the roar of the engine. 'They burn too much! Nature is a delicate thing, but they don't respect that. They only want to make money quickly and buy lots of cattle, so they burn and cut everything: fruit trees, medicine trees, trees with nuts, rubber trees, everything! I tell you, the climate is changing already. Last year we had floods because the jungle wasn't there to hold the water; we never had floods before. And the good soil is very thin and gets washed away, and then nothing grows. We must use the jungle, not just destroy it all! I am trying to do things differently, you will see.'

About thirty miles out of Porto Velho, Roberto pulled abruptly into the side and unclipped a Brazilian copy of a Winchester repeating rifle from its rack at the back of the driving cab, then he donned a grubby blue cap. 'Come,' he said to Tony. 'Something I want to show you. This is my land here; the farm is maybe another mile or less, we can go there later.'

Tony moved with an effort. He would have preferred a nap, but he could hardly refuse to follow. 'Do you always carry that thing?' he asked instead.

'What?'

'The gun.'

'Ah, the gun. Mostly yes, it's better here, just in case. Maybe there's an animal, or a man; some men are crazy, especially in the jungle.'

'Is it okay to leave my bag in the car?'

'Yes, it's fine, but best if it's out of sight maybe. Here, Senice!' Roberto called his great Dane to heel and ducked into the green gloom, which at that point was untouched right up to the road's edge.

Tony swore under his breath, and followed on uncertain legs. Had he been alone, he would have been lost within ten yards. The foliage was so thick that visibility in the green semi-light was down to about twenty feet, maximum. He stumbled painfully over hidden roots, wispy branches swiped at his face and chest, while far above the trees created a majestic canopy that completely blocked out the sun. Senice was faring little better. Beautiful he may have been, but he was no jungle dog; he was too big and ungainly.

The ground was soft and damp, and the air was never still. Leaves rustled; cicadas ground out an incessant noise interrupted occasionally by the sudden cry of a lyrical bird or raucous macaws, or the derisive laugh of a howler monkey. It was the world of the tree, massaranduba and dark jacaranda, Brazil nut trees and rubber trees, buriti and macaúba, palms of all descriptions, and ferns, mosses and lichens. Mosquitos whined and Tony slapped them away, but they were outdone by the piums, smaller than a pinhead and soundless and ever ready to gorge on plump European flesh, leaving tiny globules of blood and as painful as the prick of a needle.

Roberto appeared to be following a path of some sorts but, try as he might, Tony couldn't discern their direction. He stumbled, and was suddenly enveloped in a cloud of black bees, swatting at his head in panic. Several bees got entangled in his hair, and he suffered painful stings to his fingers pulling them out, before tripping over and falling onto the jungle loam. He watched Roberto's sweat-drenched back disappear into the gloom.

'Roberto! Where the fuck are you!'

The Brazilian reappeared, grinning. 'That, my friend, is why you always wear a hat in the jungle.'

Tony reached out to a tree to pull himself up.

'And don't touch that!' Roberto warned him. 'It's a fire tree, it will burn you if you touch it.'

'Great,' Tony muttered, his arms a mass of scratches and his shirt torn.

'It takes time to learn to walk in the jungle, it will get easier,' Roberto said. 'You must learn to walk with your eyes as well as your feet.' He held out a hand and pulled Tony to his feet. 'But you will learn to love the jungle if you stay. It is pure.'

'Hmm. Don't bet on it. How much further do we have to go?'

'Not much, ten minutes maybe.'

'English ten minutes or Brazilian?'

Roberto laughed. 'Brazilian, of course!'

He moved off again, and Tony dragged himself in pursuit. Anything was better than being abandoned in that green hell.

That Ernesto bloke in São Paulo had been right; it really was a kind of hell. As Tony forced one foot after another, swatting at piums and flies, he kept his eyes open for the odd lurking snake, scorpion or tarantula, and his ears open in case he heard the pig-like grunt of some stray alligator. He almost got to the point of cursing the madness which had induced him to even think of leaving his pointless but comfortable enough London life in the first place.

The sound of rushing water reached him not a moment too soon, the vegetation thinned, and suddenly it was light; he could see! He stood and gazed in stupefied wonder at the unexpected beauty he found himself facing. It really was a jungle paradise. A waterfall tumbled some forty feet into a limpid rock pool, huge and gaudy dragonflies swooped low over the water, delicate hummingbirds were suspended in midair, their wings beating too fast for the eye to follow, and huge butterflies with startling colours floated back and forth.

A loud splash followed by a smaller one brought him back to reality and reminded him that he was not alone. Roberto had stripped down to his underwear and was striking out with a muscular crawl towards the base of the waterfall, the faithful Senice in tow. The two of them scrambled onto a ledge of rock, and Roberto waved at Tony to follow.

Tony hesitated briefly as images of anacondas, alligators and flesh-eating piranhas flashed through his head, but then he too pulled off his boots, jeans and shirt and plunged into the water head-first, letting the cool water wash away his tiredness as he glided underneath the surface holding his breath. He finally surfaced and laughed deliriously, and moments later was perched besides Roberto and Senice. 'Oh man, this is incredible! You mean this is all yours?'

'Yes, it's mine. My border goes there across the top of the waterfall. I love it, it's my private paradise and I always want to keep it like this.'

'It's beautiful, really beautiful.'

'So, the walk was worth it, then?'

'A hundred times. Well, maybe not a hundred. But I've never seen anything like this, not in my whole life!'

'Like I told you, the jungle is beautiful if you know where to look. It's a provider, it has everything. See over there?' Roberto pointed to a clump of squat trees.

'What am I looking at?'

'They are pineapple. And there we have Brazil nuts. And there' – he kept on pointing around them – 'avocado, and banana, breadfruit, coffee and papaya. And those vines there, they have water inside that you can drink – but makes sure you pick the right one, because some of the others will poison you. You will learn.'

'What are those lumps there, on the ground?'

'The nests of termites.'

'Right. And the flowers all around, they're amazing!'

'As I said, it's my paradise, and I will keep it this way.'

Senice gave out a hoarse, half-broken bark, and Roberto threw the dog back into the water with a laugh. Tony also jumped back in, and stood under the base of the waterfall, letting the water drum onto his shoulders, giving him a crude but effective massage. Then the three of them swam lazily back to their clothes, which they donned without drying off.

'Roberto, you must have been sent to me by heaven above!' Tony told him. 'Are you sure it's okay for me to stay at your farm for a while?'

'Of course. I will enjoy the company, and it's a long time since I met anybody around here who understands beauty. People in the Amazon, they know very well how to destroy, but not how to build.' Roberto put his cap back on his head. 'So, we go?'

They must have returned by the same route, because they emerged from the forest at the exact same point at which they'd entered, by the red Ford utility, although, apart from that, no part of the stumble back struck any chord in Tony's memory.

Behind the driving wheel, Roberto rolled up a leg of his jeans and applied the lighted end of a cigarette to a small black dot above his knee.

'What are you doing?'

'It's a tick. You must be careful and get them all out; if you just pull you can leave the legs inside, and then it gets infected.' The coarse hairs on his leg burned; there was a slight smell of singed flesh, and then a tiny pop as the hard skin of the tick gave way and it dropped to the floor. Roberto grinned with satisfaction and gunned the utility into life.

CHAPTER FIVE

The Farm

After less than half a mile, the jungle to their right was cleared back to a depth of some 200 yards, much of it still charred black from recent burning. On the other side, a large fire was still in progress, thick blue-grey smoke billowing skywards to create a blood-red sunset.

Beside a small orange grove, Roberto turned into a white wooden gate. Set a short way back from the road, there was a large log ranch house, which Roberto said housed the resident cowboy, his wife and child, and the other farmhands. His own house was further in, through the orange trees: a wooden bungalow with a porch, and a veranda running the length of the front and slung with hammocks.

One of the farmhands, as dark as an African and wearing a straw hat, rubber sandals and baggy trousers, was painting the walls with black creosote, in readiness for the coming rainy season. He raised a hand and smiled a greeting to Roberto, and looked curiously at Tony. From the back of the building rose a thin spiral of smoke.

'Lourenco,' Roberto said, getting out of the Ford. 'This is my friend Tony, from England.'

Lourenco nodded a hello, then returned to his work, while Tony fetched his bag and followed Roberto and Senice into the house.

'Raimunda! Hey, Raimunda! Vir aqui!' Roberto called out, and moments later a sultry-looking girl appeared in the front room, from the kitchen area at the back. In her hand she held a large knife, presumably from chopping foodstuffs. Tony thought she had a stealthy beauty. Her eyes were liquid, as liquid as her manner; around her slender neck she wore a choker made of beads, and her thick black hair was tied back with a yellow ribbon.

'Raimunda, she lives with me,' Roberto explained. 'She doesn't speak English, not many here do.'

'I'll need to learn Brazilian, then,' Tony answered cheerfully, as he advanced and held out his hand. 'My name is Tony.'

She seemed to take his hand reluctantly; her palms were rough from work, and she carried with her a faint whiff of smoke. Then, still silent, she withdrew once more towards the back of the bungalow.

'Don't worry,' Roberto said, catching Tony's bemused look. 'You know how women are, you can't always understand them. Come, now we drink some pinga, afterwards we eat.' Roberto also went out to the back, from where Tony heard some heated argument conducted sotto voce before his newfound friend returned with a bottle of fiery sugarcane alcohol.

'You call this stuff pinga?'

'Well, the proper name is cachaça, but here we call it pinga.'

With a bowl of sliced lemons to suck after each breathtaking shot, they sat drinking in wicker chairs on the veranda, smoking and listening to the dusk crescendo of insects gathering momentum. Giant frogs croaked; cicadas ground away on membranes stretched like drumheads near their wings; grasshoppers fiddled, producing sounds with the pull of a toothed shank across the edge of their wings, while fireflies danced, glowing blue and yellow with puzzling inconsistency. Roberto lit some coils in a vain attempt to deter the mosquitos as they both sank into a pinga haze.

'It's so peaceful,' Tony remarked.

'Not so peaceful, my friend. First impressions can be deceptive.'

'Well, so far, so good. By the way, what do you call the farm?'

'Uh?'

'The name of the farm. It must have a name, doesn't it?'

'Ah, the name, yes. You know, I wish you didn't ask that! For two years I am here, and still I haven't found a name. I must find one that feels right.'

'Let's throw some ideas out, then. How about Green Hell?'

Roberto chuckled. 'No, I don't think so. I thought maybe Roberto's Ranch or Vaqueiros Hideout or something.'

'Not very inspiring,' Tony observed. He thought for a moment. 'Listen, you have the waterfall and all the flowers there, so I'm thinking how about Water Flower Garden? That has a nice ring to it. What do you think?'

'Water Flower Garden?' Roberto knitted his brows, then opened his eyes wide. 'Water Flower Garden! Yes, I like that! It represents peace and beauty, I think the pinga must be good for you! Tomorrow I will make a sign. Welcome to Water Flower Garden! Now let's eat.'

CHAPTER SIX

THE SHERIFF

Tony slept on the veranda in a double hammock slung from beams across the front doorway, which was the prime place given that it got the full benefit of any through-draught. The space inside the four walls was intolerably hot and airless.

Sleeping in a hammock, though, is not an art discovered in a single night. Tony hadn't learned yet that the best way to get comfortable was to lie diagonally, and wrap the rest of the hammock around you as much as possible to keep out the blood-sucking insects.

For a habitual face-down sleeper like Tony it was a struggle. Several times his body turned over of its own accord during the night, leaving him bent the wrong way, and more than once he capsized, tipping onto the hard floor. But the pinga and exhaustion had done their work, and in time he fell unconscious, hunched up on his back in the pit of the hammock, oblivious even to the torturous mosquitos.

He awoke barely refreshed to a transparent dawn just a few hours later, his back aching, neck stiff and sore, and every visible patch of skin swollen with large red mosquito bites which itched mercilessly. He shuffled from the porch to a nearby trough of water and ducked his head under, then gave a rudimentary wash to the rest of his body. Roberto appeared soon after, little livelier, a white towel wrapped around his hips, and they crouched together in the shade of an orange tree watching the already hot day come on quickly, the dawn chorus of insects producing such a different sound from their dusk counterparts, somehow more mellow and less intrusive.

'So, Tony, how are you feeling?'

'All right. No, on second thoughts, bloody awful. What have you done to me?'

'I am the same, but I have something to make it better. Let's go into the house.'

There was a front room half the length of the veranda, with partition walls to make three other rooms: the kitchen, a bedroom, and a bathroom with a generator-powered shower along with a claw-footed bathtub. The floor was concrete, and most of the furnishings, such as they were – a dining table with four chairs, a rocking chair, and a couple of chests for storage – were made from local hardwood. In the simple kitchen, which had a small open fire and a shuttered window looking out over a banana grove, Roberto grated a lump of speckled rock-like substance into a plastic cup, before adding a spoon of sugar and water from a stone jar.

'Here,' he said, 'drink it all in one go.'

Tony tossed the mixture back and made a face. 'Yeuch! What is that?'

'Guarana, it's a root from the jungle. I take it every morning, it's very good for you, gives you energy. Next, we drink some maté.' Roberto offered Tony a small gourd with a spoon-shaped silver straw. 'It's hot, but it's also good for you, also gives you energy. It's like a green tea.'

'Anything else for breakfast? Or is that it?'

'Next, we have some coffee, and maybe a banana or some bread. We don't have big breakfasts here like you do in England, but we have a good lunch, and then a siesta.'

Tony felt he could have wished for something a bit more substantial, some eggs maybe, but then again, he was already feeling better, and it was already getting very hot, so maybe a big breakfast wasn't what he needed. He took his thick, sweet black coffee back to the porch and sat in one of the wicker chairs. Roberto joined him soon afterwards.

'You smoke grass, Tony?'

'Er, I have done, sometimes. Why?'

Roberto produced a small plastic bag. 'Colombian. It's the best, much better than Brazilian.' He began to roll a small joint. 'It will make you feel better.'

'You mean take the energy away again? I've only just started to feel something like normal!'

'Life is slow here. Too much energy is not so good.'

Roberto lit up, and Tony accepted the proffered smoke, thinking that surely just a little could do no harm, perhaps just take the edge off the day. Seconds later his mind went numb and the insects seemed to turn the volume up to a deafening roar.

'You like it?'

'I'll let you know when I can think again. Hell, this stuff is strong!'

'You have grass in England?'

'Well, mostly hashish, there is some grass, but not like this!'

'Many people here smoke,' Roberto told him. 'There's no need to be fast. Like I said, life here is slow, very slow. Anyway, I go to dress, then we visit the sheriff.'

'We visit the what?' Tony asked, appalled.

'The sheriff, he lives near here.'

'Can't it wait? I mean, look what you've done to me, Roberto: guilty at a hundred paces at least! My eyes must be redder than, well, I don't know, the planet Mars!'

'Don't worry, he's not the police.' Roberto chuckled. 'He's a friend of mine.'

'You're sure?'

'Of course!'

'What about me getting back to Porto Velho?'

'You don't want to stay here?'

'Well, yes, but it feels like a bit of an imposition.'

'Nonsense. If you want to stay, then stay!'

'What about Raimunda?'

'She's not here, she's gone out already.'

'But I get the impression she's not too happy to have me here.'

Roberto shrugged. 'Ah, you know women, my friend. She will get used to it. Women always want too much; most of the time I don't really understand them.'

'How do you mean?'

'To begin with, they say one thing, but they mean another. They try to change you, and when you don't change, they start to hate you. It's like they want you all to themselves, and their memories! Every little thing stored away to be used after you've long forgotten whatever it was that happened. They can be beautiful, but they can be infuriating too.'

Tony chuckled. 'As the old saying goes, can't live with them, can't live without them. Come on, then, let's go.'

They drove a mile or so down the road and slid to a dusty halt besides a long wooden hut. They ducked in through the low doorway to be met inside by a cheerful middle-aged man with a huge stomach straining under a white vest, his trousers held up by braces, with twinkling eyes and thinning grey hair. He was standing behind a tiny bar, the walls behind lined with musty-looking cans of Brahma Chopp, some imported lagers, and bottles of Coca-Cola and Fanta. From the ceiling hung plastic bags of dried fish and meat, safe from the marauding insects below.

'O, Roberto!' the man greeted them.

'O, José! Vou apresentá-lo a meo amigo, Tony. O Inglês.'

'O Inglês?' José held out a podgy hand, his eyes smiling warmly. 'Encantado! Quanto tempo vai estar aqui?'

'He asks how long you stay,' Roberto translated.

Tony shrugged.

'Fala Português?' José still held on to his hand, a lingering handshake, slow like everything else.

'Nâo, sómente um poco.' Tony turned to Roberto. 'Tell him I'm learning!'

José laughed out loud, holding his plump stomach as if it was the best joke he'd heard in years, then spoke rapidly to Roberto. Tony only managed to decipher the word 'Inglês' several times.

'What's he saying now?'

'He talks about the railway the English built in Porto Velho, many years ago. But actually, I don't think it was the English; I'm not sure. Maybe the Americans.'

'There's a railway? I didn't see one!'

'It was from Porto Velho to the border with Bolivia. It stopped working a few years ago. Above Porto Velho there are a lot of waterfalls, the river is not navigable, so they built a railway for more than 200 miles from Porto Velho to Guajará-Mirim to get around the waterfalls. José says that many people died building it, but it was a magnificent railway. Most of the old railway route we now use as a road.'

'Amazing. Well, tell him the railways hardly work anymore in England either!'

Roberto translated, and they all chuckled. 'I'm sure that not true,' Roberto said, 'but you English seem to have been everywhere, and then when you left, there was hardly a footprint. Unlike the Spanish or Portuguese.'

José served them a bottle of Brahma Chopp each from his fridge, then seemed to lapse back into an Amazonian inertia, just waiting and watching. He sprinkled some poisoned pink sugar crystals onto the bar and watched absentmindedly as a cloud of flies took the bait, then flicked their corpses away with a finger once the poison had done its work.

'This guy is really a sheriff?' Tony asked Roberto.

'Yes, he really is, but it means nothing really. Does it, José?'

The unlikely sheriff looked up again at the mention of his name and languidly changed his position. He launched into a long monologue, moving his arms through the air as if through water, and drawing incomprehensible diagrams between the dead flies on the bar with the puddles from their beers.

'What was that all about?' Tony asked.

Roberto smiled. 'He says he has lived here all his life and had nothing, and then the road came and it is making him rich.'

Tony glanced at the wide red scar running past the hut, the empty cans littering the dusty ground. It was sweltering out there now, so hot even the chickens were panting. 'Rich' struck him as perhaps something of an overstatement, but José seemed to think that one day, maybe, if you waited long enough, the promised land would deliver. Tony was beginning to understand the Amazon dream.

CHAPTER SEVEN

Pitanga

Tony stayed on at Water Flower Garden almost by accident, one day slipping unnoticed into another. Money wasn't a problem; he had a lump sum in the bank from the sale of his London apartment and division of assets after his divorce, and he didn't need much. Occasionally he thought he should perhaps move on, but Roberto always dissuaded him.

Tony worked as hard as anyone on the farm, his skin losing its soft milky appearance and taking on the yellowy leather hue of a tropical tan. He learned the curious glottal tongue of the typical Amazonian, the dropping of adverbs and pronouns, and the saudade of the people, the sad yearning. He even began to sleep comfortably in a hammock.

The only part of the farm's life that he studiously avoided was the visits to the local slaughterhouse on a neighbouring property. It was primitive in the extreme: a white tiled box where scrawny cattle waited in restless fear in a corral outside, wide-eyed from the stench of fresh blood, a sweet sick smell, and the screams of their former companions who were already being put to the knife. The animals were lassoed one by one and dragged into the killing zone, where Lourenco, stripped to the waist and his black skin glistening, delivered a paralysing knife thrust to the base of the skull. If the victim didn't die from the blade, other workers set about clubbing it to death, then skinning and butchering it, while doe-eyed youths poured buckets of water over the carcass to keep the myriad flies at bay. On the branches of the trees outside, black-hooded urubu, vulture scavengers, waited in their hundreds, hoping for scraps.

Tony felt sure the method of killing was one of the reasons the meat they ate was always so tough and chewy, the release of adrenaline by the terrified animals increasing the muscle tension. He was sure he'd read something to that effect back home as an argument for more humane methods of slaughter, and passed his thoughts on to Roberto. Together they agreed to look into the economics of investing in equipment to stun the cattle first, and whether it could be a service they offered to other nearby farms to recoup the expense.

Most of the days were a mix of clearing back new land by machete – Roberto rarely resorted to fire – branding cattle, checking the wire fencing around the new fields, making sure the fruit trees were free of infestation, paying visits to José and other neighbours to drink thick sweet coffee and enjoy an idle exchange of gossip, and an almost daily swim at the waterfall. The name of Water Flower Garden was painted in crude white letters on a wooden slat and nailed above the front porch. By the time evening came, Tony was always tired, his muscles aching, but it was a welcome tiredness and his mind was at ease. He was happy.

One day as Tony and Roberto swung in hammocks on the veranda, escaping from the heat of the day after lunch, Roberto suddenly sat up and waved. 'Hey, it's Pitanga! Olá Pitanga! This is someone you must meet. Sometimes he works on the farm here, but he is an Indio, from the Karitiana tribe.'

'This I must see,' Tony said, dangling his legs over the edge of the hammock. 'I thought that the Indians were few and far between these days?'

'Yes, many have died. There's only a few hundred Karitiana left and they rarely come out of the jungle, but Pitanga is different.'

Pitanga arrived beside them, a shy smile on his almost Asiatic face. He was a small man, with hairless light brown skin, and narrow eyes which were fringed with few lashes. He had an inquisitive look, and there was a childlike quality about his movements. On his wrist he wore a homemade bracelet made from the remains of red and white Coca-Cola cans, and around his neck he had a delicate necklace fashioned out of small teeth. Tony asked about the necklace, and the question prompted a lengthy story which, because of Pitanga's own peculiar adaptation of Portuguese, Roberto had to translate as they went along.

'He says,' Roberto began, 'that a long time ago, a Karitiana man decided to make some necklaces, so he and some friends crossed the river to look for suitable ornaments. The man was at the back of the group as they waded through the water, when suddenly a huge jacaré – it's like a crocodile – caught him and swallowed him whole. His friends were sad. "A jacaré ate our friend!" they said, and they returned home and told the other people in the village what had happened. By this time, it was getting late, and dark.'

Pitanga looked sorrowful for a moment, then brightened up and began talking again. 'Meanwhile, inside the jacaré, the man suddenly thought, *Where is my little basket?* and he searched and found it. Inside he had some piranha teeth, and he took these and began to cut at the jacaré's intestines, until he opened up the stomach, and the jacaré began to thrash the water with his tail because of the pain. The man kept cutting away at the animal's insides until he reached the heart, which he also cut. "I think it is dying now," the man said to himself, and then he heard a scraping sound as the beast dragged itself onto a beach and lay down. The man then cut a hole by its ribs and daylight flooded in, and he came out into the sunshine. He was *so* cold, so he lay down by a tree to warm up.' Pitanga shook himself to show what it was like to be cold, enjoying his story, then went on.

'Later, the man returned to his village and told them what had happened, and everyone was *amazed*! "If I hadn't had my piranha teeth with me, I would never have got out," he told them, and he sat down in the sunlight, still cold and trembling. His hair had fallen out and his head had become white.' Pitanga came to the end of his story and smiled, fingering his necklace.

'So those are piranha teeth?' Tony asked. 'Is that why he wears them, then?'

'Yes, it is the custom with all the men of his tribe,' Roberto explained.

'It's a bit like the story of Jonah and the whale!'

'I don't know that story.'

'Well, it's about a guy who gets swallowed by a whale. I can't remember how he got out, but he did after a few days. Actually, I think it's a religious story; maybe God saved him. Anyway, same sort of thing.'

Pitanga started talking again, pointing at distant fires.

'He's asking if you would like to hear another story, this time about fire,' Roberto said. 'Indios love to tell stories.'

'Sure, yes, please tell him to go ahead.'

Pitanga began talking rapidly, stringing words together as if he were singing a song, and again Roberto had to translate.

'He says that long ago, the fire ate a man called O-Hay. O-Hay was a silly person; when people spoke to him, he didn't believe any of them, so the fire ate him up. The people had told O-Hay that when the fire burns a field, you must not look, but he went up a tree and watched the fire from far away. But the fire came quickly to the place where O-Hay was and jumped to the top of the tree and ate him, and afterwards all that was left of him was charcoal.'

Pitanga took another of his pauses, shaking his head and looking sad, then continued.

'After a while, an old man from the village said, "Let's go and see how the fire went," and so they did, and they found the fire crying and crying. "Oh, what's the matter, respected friend?" they asked. And the fire replied, "I ate O-Hay," and then the fire began to sing, "O-Hay nya, ititnakatdyer, O-Hay nya, ititnakatdyer, murra, taka, hopi, sou na," which means, "If there should be a son of O-Hay, if there should be a son of O-Hay, he is mine, so he won't be thin." And then, still crying, the fire went away.'

Pitanga said something else, then fell silent.

'Is that it?' Tony asked, bemused.

'Yes, and he says that now the Karitiana still sing this song when they go hunting or into their fields. It's called "The Child of the Fire". In the old days, Pitanga says they never had to light a fire; it always came to them when they called it with this song, but otherwise it never bothered them.'

'Great story! Obrigado, Pitanga,' Tony thanked him.

'Nada.' He made a small bow and moved off through the fruit trees, singing softly to himself in his own language.

'You will not meet many Indians like Pitanga,' Roberto said. 'He is lucky; he lives on my land in the jungle. It's not really allowed, but he is happy and I don't mind.'

'What do you mean, he's lucky?'

'Because when tribes are discovered, the government tries to teach them to be like us, and the missionaries move in and try to convert them to Christianity, and they forget who they are, their culture dies. In the end, most of them drink too much pinga, and if they have some good land someone always tries to take it away.'

'That's sad. Where's the rest of his tribe?'

'About one hundred kilometres from here, further up the Madeira River, near the border with Bolivia. Most of them stay hidden in the jungle, but some have been rehoused in government-built malocas; it's a copy of a traditional longhouse, but they are lost there.'

'It makes me angry, you know? Indigenous people always seem to get fucked over,' Tony told him. 'Look at America, look at Australia, hey, even the Zulus fucked over the Bushmen in South Africa, but you guys had a chance to do something differently. All I've seen in the Amazon is destruction. Why can't these guys be left alone?'

'You're right. In theory they have large areas of the forest set aside for them, and they live with nature, they don't fight it. But in the end, money always wins, and if someone wants the land that belongs to the Indios, for a mine or something, they usually get it.'

CHAPTER EIGHT

A Dark Cloud

Roberto and Tony visited the waterfall most evenings to cool off and wash the grime from their bodies, to watch the sun sink low in a smoke-filled sky. It really was like a secret paradise, but there was a hidden menace too: by its very beauty, the waterfall represented danger.

One evening they sat on the ledge by the base of the waterfall, watching a blue-headed kingfisher diving without warning into the crystal water, while Senice snapped and yelped vainly after huge erratic butterflies. Tony gazed at the pool's bottom, where grey fish glided over polished stones, round and white like prehistoric eggs. 'You can really be alone here, can't you?' he murmured.

'You can't ever be sure that you're alone. You don't know who might be watching,' Roberto answered.

Tony looked around, but saw nothing to disturb the calm of the moment. 'What do you mean? You think we're being watched now?'

'I don't think so, but you can't be sure.' Roberto sighed and pushed his black hair back from his face. 'Ever since I was a child, I have loved the jungle. One day I will take you for a long trek in the forest, two or maybe three weeks. It's beautiful, there's a strength in it, and after many days you smell of the jungle. That's why I don't want to destroy everything, but it means I have enemies too.'

'Enemies? Isn't there enough for everybody here?'

'For some there is never enough. You know the farm on the other side of the road from mine?'

'Rio Novo? Yes, you never go there, do you? Is he your enemy, then? Tony was perplexed, and wondered why the question had never occurred to him before.

'He would like to kill me.' Roberto turned to look his friend in the eyes.

'Kill you?'

'Because he wants to have the waterfall. His land is at the top,' and he turned to point to where the water gushed out above their heads. 'He wants to build a road here and make a hotel.'

'That's mad; who the fuck needs a hotel out here?'

'One day this will be a rich place.' Roberto turned back. 'The Amazon is all about the future. Maybe in ten or twenty years, but one day, and then many people will come here.'

'And you think this guy would kill you for that? What's his name?'

'De Brito. Marcus de Brito. He's a Paulista.'

'From São Paulo?'

'Yes.'

'So, what will you do?'

'I can do nothing, only watch and wait, and try to move faster than him, and of course hope my jeito is better than his.'

'Your what?'

'Jeito. It's a Brazilian thing, it's difficult to explain, but it's like the gift of knowing a thing before it happens.'

'Like a sixth sense?'

'Yes, like that. Once before he tried to burn the land here, but I managed to put the flames out. He said it was a mistake, fires get out of control all the time, but it wasn't a mistake. You can see for yourself, there is no law here. A man has to fight to protect what is his.'

Tony shivered, but it wasn't from cold, and he found himself scanning the surrounding forest again for unseen eyes. 'That's why you carry the gun?'

Roberto shrugged. 'It's better that I do. There are too many bad men here who will kill for money, pistoleiros. I have seen peasants burnt alive in their homes because someone else wanted their land. It's a wild place.'

'Fuck!' Tony's good mood had evaporated. 'But if you're sure this guy is out to kill you, why not act first? Kill him, even.' Even as he said it, he thought it sounded absurd, but it turned out it was something Roberto had already considered.

'Once I planned to. I thought I would bury his body in the jungle and fly to Bolivia, come back later. They would never catch me.'

'Why didn't you?'

'Because it is not a good way.' Roberto spread his arms out. 'There will always be someone else, and I don't want to start the killing. If I have to, I will do it, but I hope it's not necessary.'

'If it comes to a fight, I'll have your back,' Tony declared. 'You know that, don't you?'

'It's not your fight, amigo. But enough of this talk; it's time for a pinga. I race you back!'

CHAPTER NINE

Fazenda Rio Novo

Marcus de Brito was a Paulista who had bought the Rio Novo some five years earlier, and Roberto was right: he did have big plans for the farm. He had just turned fifty years old and wore his blond hair cropped short, above a pinched face with grey and watery eyes.

His ruthless streak had gained him a notoriety even in the dog-eat-dog world of São Paulo, where he'd begun life as an abandoned orphan and, growing up, had scraped a living as a shoeshine boy, kneeling at the feet of people he both envied and hated. Sometimes, when times were extra hard, he'd sell himself to those people too, which fed his loathing of them and himself. He hated them so much that he had become one of them, without feeling, but now the extent of his wealth was anybody's guess. After a string of land deals in the new world – some barely legal, others very illegal – and, it has to be said, some killings, first on behalf of others and later for himself, he had amassed a personal fortune that could be reckoned to be at least in multiple millions of US dollars.

He still spent most of his time in São Paulo, but now, instead of being down on one knee, juggling shoeshine brushes with artful dexterity, he enjoyed the privacy of a mansion in the upmarket western district of Morumbi. He liked the area because it was close to the headquarters of the state governor, someone who needed to be kept onside with regular bribes, and it boasted several major hospitals, along with the Jockey Club and the University of São Paulo, which provided ample green spaces. The district was also a classic example of the inequalities in the city, given that it was surrounded by slums, which reminded de Brito of where he had come from, and where he had no intention of going back.

To a man like him, the Amazon meant only one thing: money. He'd lobbied hard back in the late fifties for the rainforest to be opened up, and it had been a prayer answered when the military seized power in 1964, given that they shared his views on attacking the rainforest. He had even been one of the principal advocates for the craziest of all Amazon schemes: to dam the mouth of the river and attempt to flood the entire forest, killing all the trees, and then drain the vast area again to create farmland. The idea was shelved when someone pointed out that the Amazon represented about a quarter of the world's remaining green matter, a whole half of the world's rainforests, and, as it is vegetation that supplies our oxygen, the elimination of so much forest overnight could theoretically lead to the suffocation of all breathing beings, man and beast.

In the end, the colonisation of Amazonia had been geared to roads, notably the Trans-Amazonian Highway, 2,000 miles of red dust with tributary roads running off at angles. Wherever there was a road, peasant homesteaders, many taken from the big cities' slums and forcibly resettled, would be cutting and burning. But, while Amazonia is ideal territory for insects, plants, reptiles and other wildlife, it is not an easy place to live for humans, and developing it soon started costing a lot of money. Billions of dollars had evaporated, but still the surface of the forest was barely scratched.

In the late 1960s, when the big rush was starting to gather momentum, de Brito acquired parcels of land wherever there was a whisper of a new road to be built. If there were squatters or Indians on the land, they weren't there when he resold it to the Americans, Japanese, Germans and Swiss. But of late he'd sunk a sizeable portion of his fortune into a share of a massive development off the road from Santarém to Cuiabá, a project which included the creation of an entirely new town, and which he expected was going to provide him with a huge return on investment.

The Rio Novo farm was, therefore, a comparatively minor concern to de Brito from a business perspective for the time being, a jungle retreat for the future when the region was a bit more civilised, and he visited Porto Velho only occasionally, for a couple of days at a time. One day he hoped to spend a lot of time there, after he'd built a magnificent jungle palace to live in. For that, Roberto was right to say that he wanted the waterfall, but it wasn't so he could put a hotel there. Rather, his vision was an exotic complex for himself and esteemed guests only, a kind of legacy to himself.

In the meantime, Rio Novo, with its log bungalow like all its neighbours, had been left under the supervision of an indolent and bullying ruffian called Vincente. He was a pig-fat man with a permanent growth of three to four days' worth of facial hair, beetle eyebrows, a hooked nose and a jagged scar on his neck, probably from a bullet. He lorded it over a motley band of teenagers, and an ancient cook who prepared pots of beefy for breakfast, lunch and dinner, and he was constantly fighting with the farm manager, Adriano, a bearded and wiry young man from Maranhão with a happy and enthusiastic way.

Each week, as part of his duties, Vincente had to drive the half-hour into Porto Velho to use the telephone at the post office and report that everything was in order to de Brito. And every three months, if the boss wasn't visiting, he'd have to wash and shave, don a shirt and tie, and board the morning flight to São Paulo to report in person.

Tony's presence at Water Flower Garden was therefore quickly noted and reported.

'Sim, a gringo jefe, really, I make no mistake!' Vincente squeaked excitedly down the telephone line in his high-pitched voice.

Fifteen hundred miles to the southeast, de Brito's face darkened. 'A gringo, you say? What is he doing there?'

'I don't know. He has been working, but he won't stay for long; no one ever does, especially a foreigner.'

'Keep me informed. I will let you know when I can come up.' De Brito slammed his receiver back into place.

Tony couldn't be anything but a threat to his plans; no doubt the gringo was a friend of that sentimental fool Roberto. But still, with a gringo one had to be discreet. De Brito closed his eyes and leaned back in his soft, black leather office chair and thought.

By coincidence, it was the same day that Roberto gave Tony a pistol. 'You can borrow it while you are here; you should not be unarmed.'

It was an almost new Smith & Wesson Model 19, small and light: a wheel gun that held six bullets, with a double action trigger and a polished nickel barrel. Tony weighed the gun in his hand. 'But I don't even know how to use it!'

'We will practise; I have plenty of bullets. It's an easy gun to learn. And anyway, probably you will never have to use it, but it's better to have, just in case.' He also gave Tony a piece of paper with a name and an address on it, along with a telephone number. 'My mother, in Rio Grande do Sul,' he said. 'Just in case.'

Tony wondered, if push came to shove, whether he'd ever actually be able to pull the trigger in anger.

CHAPTER TEN

Rain

The heavens finally opened near the end of December. For several weeks dark clouds had been gathering, threatening rain, and the air became oppressive. Then suddenly one night it came crashing down, drumming deafeningly on the corrugated roof of the bungalow, waking everyone up. Roberto and Tony sat on the veranda, smoking and watching the curtain of water pouring down. Even Raimunda joined them for a while, before disappearing to make coffee for them all.

As Ernesto had promised in São Paulo, the rain fell near-constantly for four months. Occasionally it eased off, but then the downpour would resume with even more ferocity. During the heaviest downpours, there was little they could do except watch and wait. The air became so thick with damp it would have been no surprise to see fish swimming in through the door, and the red scar highway dissolved into a river of mud, as they huddled in the bungalow like shipwrecked sailors.

Their moods varied between long days of incredible stupor, almost to the point of hallucination, and short periods of startling lucidity. Nothing was dry, not their clothes, the bedsheets or towels. Green mould started to appear on the walls, and Tony became thinner while his hair grew longer.

On the days when the rain wasn't torrential, Tony and Roberto made regular forays into the jungle; the overhead canopy acted like a giant umbrella, but everything dripped. Tony learnt how to walk in the jungle, making high careful steps and always with his eyes open – and his head covered. He came to recognise the giant sloth edging its way painfully slowly along tree branches, the screech of a macaw or jeering monkeys, along with the rat-tailed armadillo, coatis – cat-sized mammals native to the jungle – tapirs and opossums. Once Roberto reached into the undergrowth and dragged out a young anaconda: he said it was only about a year old, but it was a good six feet long, and Tony could only imagine how large it would be when fully grown.

On other days they drove into Porto Velho to stock up on supplies and try to learn news of anything interesting, but the town, like the forest, was subdued during the rains.

Then, in the middle of January, Tony went down with malaria, spending two weeks drenched in sweat while shivering uncontrollably. At times he was delirious; his back ached, and there was a constant dull throb at the base of his skull. The skin on his hands and feet began to rot and peel off, and the pounds of flesh literally fell away until he was almost skeletal.

Raimunda nursed him with broths of chicken and beans and jungle herbs, but there was nothing else to do except to wait the fever out, until finally it did break. For the first time in two weeks, he struggled to his feet and sat in a chair on the veranda.

'You need to take it easy,' Roberto told him. 'The malaria can stay in the body for a long time, and often it comes back. Maybe not so strong, but it is inside of you now.'

Tony nodded weakly. 'I guess it's like our winter flu back home; every year it comes back. But I'm over the malaria now, just need to get my strength back.'

The next day he shaved off his fortnight's growth of beard and moustache, nicking himself several times with the cutthroat razor, given that his hands were still trembling slightly, but happy with the outcome. But his hair, now bleached by the sun, he decided to leave shoulder-length.

*

When the rains ended, the deluge ceased almost as suddenly as it had begun, the burning sun once again taking control of the skies, drying the road and signalling the new dry season, when the work of burning and slashing could begin anew.

A year passed, then two, and then another. Tony no longer thought about when he might leave; he had made his home there, literally. Together with Roberto he had built a small second bungalow on the farm, which he now inhabited, along with a darkly beautiful woman he'd struck up with in Porto Velho. Her name was Conceição, which meant 'immaculate', and for Tony she was, with long black hair that reached her slim waist, and a ready smile. Her father had been a small farmer but had passed away several years before. Her mother had subsequently abandoned her for another man, and Conceição had survived by waitressing and doing cleaning jobs, until she met Tony, who had come to eat at the restaurant where she was working and was immediately smitten.

Tony was by now fully conversant in the local variety of Brazilian Portuguese and, like the locals, had taken to dressing in baggy trousers and a cotton shirt, topped by a straw hat. Even his manner had become more like one of the locals, a sort of sad yearning typical of the Amazon, until the natives themselves occasionally forgot that he was really a gringo in disguise.

Together they painted their small home a bright yellow, and Roberto soon copied them to do the same for the main bungalow. They laid flower beds in front of both buildings, and planted dahlias, hollyhock and brilliant marigolds. They also planted fields of corn, pineapples, beans and manioc, the local staple diet. Away to one side, they constructed a small corral with a corrugated iron roof and surrounded by chicken wire, where two goats, a pig and some brown hens lived in peaceful communion. In time, Water Flower Garden became known far and wide for its astonishing beauty and apparent tranquillity; the way it blended with the forest, representing a tribute to nature instead of an ugly scar on the earth's face like most of its neighbours.

But, although on the surface all appeared calm and peaceful, there was a dark side too. Rio Novo continued to represent an undercurrent of violence, always there but never quite erupting. Until it did.

CHAPTER ELEVEN

A Meeting

It was shortly after the end of Tony's third rainy season that they noticed de Brito had started spending a lot more time over at Rio Novo. He was always accompanied by a feral-looking henchman called Francisco, who wore a pistol on one side and a machete on the other: a thin-faced man with a pencil moustache, who never seemed to smile.

Roberto and Tony knew everything that happened at Rio Novo because Adriano kept them informed. The two of them were surprised, however, when a dreamy-eyed barefoot boy interrupted their dusk pinga ritual on the veranda one day with an invitation for them to have dinner with de Brito across the road.

'He wants something,' Roberto said. 'I won't be going. If he wants something, he can come here himself and ask for it.'

'Wow, you really don't like him, do you?'

'I know him. Go and see for yourself if you like.'

'Okay, I will. Someone's got to talk sometime!' Tony stood up. 'Better go and take a shower, then.'

'Just be careful.'

As the sun disappeared, Tony walked over to Rio Novo in a clean, crisp white shirt, and cotton slacks. He was met at the gate by a surly Francisco and led into the main building, where de Brito was waiting with Adriano, who shook Tony by the hand.

De Brito wasn't put out that Roberto had declined to attend. In fact, he was pleased; it was the gringo he was interested in. He handed Tony a glass of lukewarm Moselle white wine. 'I'm sorry it's not cold,' he rasped. 'This place is quite uncivilised, but with luck the cook has prepared something almost edible tonight. Please, take a seat.'

The table was crudely hewn mahogany, and the chairs were hard. Candles and a kerosene lamp provided the only light, the dancing shadows playing tricks with Tony's eyes. He sat at the table with de Brito and Adriano, while Francisco remained in the corner of the room, watching, as the cook served up a concoction of fish and rice which was less than appetising.

'So, tell me.' De Brito turned to Tony. 'What exactly is a gringo doing out here, in the middle of nowhere?'

'I'm not a gringo, I'm English.'

As with Ernesto in São Paulo, this earned him a shrug. 'There's no difference. But okay, Englishman, tell me why you are here.'

Tony prodded his food, and hoped there would be some leftovers from dinner at Water Flower Garden. 'Not sure I can give you a precise answer to that.' He looked directly into the eyes of the other man, which were glittering with malice, while Adriano fiddled nervously with his knife and fork, looking from one to the other with darting eyes. The room was hot and airless, so the sweat prickled at Tony's back. Coming here had been a mistake, he thought. 'But I can tell you that I'm happy here, I came here to make a new start, on a whim, really; I needed to get away from London. I didn't expect to stay this long, but here I am! What about you? What are your plans for Rio Novo?'

'That is my concern, not yours.' De Brito watched him with unblinking eyes, like a bird of prey. 'But one day I will build something beautiful here, with air conditioning, a swimming pool.'

'That sounds nice.' Tony had given up on the food; it was revolting.

'But life can be difficult here, even dangerous,' De Brito continued softly.

'That's what I've been told.'

'A man must be careful.'

'I try to be.'

'And his papers must be in order, especially a foreigner.'

'I think you'll find mine are completely in order.' Tony was beginning to feel uncomfortable under de Brito's unflinching stare and the silent threat of Francisco. Adriano fidgeted, but took no part in the conversation.

Finally, after what seemed like an eternity, the cook removed their plates. De Brito poured some more of the warm wine for Tony. 'Dessert? Coffee, perhaps?'

'I really must be going, I'm afraid, things to do, but thanks for the wine; it's been a pleasure.' Tony rose from his place and de Brito stood with him.

'So soon? Perhaps we will have another chance?' He held out his bony hand for Tony to shake. It was like touching marble.

'Yes, perhaps.'

'That is, if you decide to stay longer in Porto Velho. As I said, a man must be careful.'

'Yes, yes, I heard that. Goodnight, then.'

Tony said farewell to Adriano as well, and took his leave. Outside he breathed the air deeply and, despite the warmth of the night, he shivered. He crossed the road and walked back through the orange grove, glancing back over his shoulder more than once to see Francisco standing sentinel at the gates of Rio Novo.

CHAPTER TWELVE

Fire

By now, Water Flower Garden boasted some 200 head of cattle grazing in fields of spiky grass, along with their fruit and vegetable plots. The farm was beginning to turn a profit, and Tony had researched the establishment of a more humane abattoir. He still had his share of the proceeds from the sale of his flat in London virtually untouched, so he was not short of funds and could invest part of the money in the project. Roberto and a small loan from a bank in Porto Velho would provide the rest.

One day, Tony was trotting a stunted white stallion back from the fields with Lourenco's son Enzo, a tiny replica of his father on his own pony, when he spotted Adriano drinking coffee with Lourenco's wife Teresa in the farmhands' ranch house. He dismounted and went to join them, while Enzo scurried away to pull buckets of water from the well for the lathering horses.

'Olá, Adriano; olá, Teresa,' he called out as he opened the wooden gate to the square concrete-floored living room, which was more of a patio with two walls only half height and open to the outside. He set himself down at the basic table and helped himself to a couple of fingers' worth of sweet black coffee. 'What news?'

Adriano shrugged, his customary easy-going manner absent. 'Rio Novo.' He jerked a thumb over his shoulder, while Teresa, a mountain of a woman so large you couldn't see the stool she was sitting on, twiddled the knobs on a red plastic transistor radio with fading batteries. 'De Brito is spending a lot of time up here now, you know. He's making a lot of work, as if he's in a hurry. He doesn't understand, you can't hurry the Amazon. You saw the bulldozer?'

'The big yellow Komatsu?'

'Yes, he's clearing a lot of land. Up near your waterfall too.'

'You're kidding!'

'I'm not; you should go and see. He's up to something. I don't know what, because he won't tell me, but he's a dangerous man. I will have to leave Rio Novo soon, otherwise I think I will have trouble with him. It's why I don't come here so often now.' Adriano rose to leave. 'Adeus, Teresa.'

'You take care, young man from Maranhão,' she answered as he planted a wide-brimmed hat made from cow hide on his head.

Tony went to look for Roberto to tell him what he'd heard from Adriano. Then they went together to the waterfall, climbing up to the top, where they found trees uprooted and a large space cleared, with a new track made by the bulldozer leading back to Rio Novo. 'The bastard is up to something,' Roberto muttered. 'We need to watch our backs.'

The next day Roberto went to Porto Velho and had his lawyer draw up a detailed land title for Water Flower Garden, with a map precisely spelling out the farm's boundaries. During the following fortnight, he and Tony and all the farmhands worked to finish the fencing around the farm's boundaries, digging the stakes deep into the ground. With machetes, they cut a narrow path through the forest to the waterfall, which they also fenced off, including at the top. It seemed a shame to desecrate the place in this way, but Roberto insisted they had to put down a marker: draw their line in the jungle, as it were.

They still swam regularly in the clear water, with the huge polished stones and gaudy butterflies, but it felt different now. Roberto had become watchful and tense, never far from his rifle. When a howler monkey laughed it seemed to be mocking them, the screech of a macaw became a yell of alarm, and always they had a feeling of unseen eyes following their every move from the jungle.

'It's getting to be like the fucking Cold War,' Tony said as he lay on a rock near the water's edge examining enormous clicking ants, the late afternoon sun warm on his back, his skin spotted with dots of blood from the murderous piums.

Roberto started cleaning his Winchester copy. 'The Amazon is a waiting world, my friend. There's not much we can do but watch, and wait. A couple of years is not long to wait here.'

'Wouldn't it be better to take the fight to him? Confront him?'

'That's what he wants. De Brito is a powerful man with a lot of money; he can bribe people. We need to be above reproach.'

Tony stood up, restless. 'Fair enough, I understand that. But in a way it'd be nice to have some action soon; that's if there's going to be any action. This waiting game is getting on my tits.'

'You're not wearing your gun,' Roberto pointed out as he snapped the rifle shut and sighted on a bright blue toucan halfway up a tree, without firing.

'You're right, I left it behind by mistake. Still haven't quite got used to packing a gun all the time, but I should. Otherwise, if it all kicks off, I'd not be much use.'

'Be patient a little longer. I'm convinced de Brito will try something soon. If he's going to do anything, it will be before the next rainy season.'

'Well, okay, you know better than me.' Tony reached down for a stick, which he threw into the water. 'Hey, Senice, race you for it!'

Senice was a good swimmer, but not as fast as Tony, who reached the stick first and threw it again, then turned and swam back to the rocks, panting happily from the exertion. He pushed back his dripping hair and arched his spine, giving his face the full benefit of the dying sun rays.

'Come on, let's go,' Roberto said. 'It'll be dark soon, and this is probably not the best place to be in the dark.'

They returned to the houses along the narrow path they had created, the green jungle dark above their heads, climbing lianas and cascading vines, cicadas grinding then falling suddenly silent, startled by their human footfall. The perfumes of the forest were especially strong in the evening, as if the whole jungle was breathing a sigh of relief at the close of another broiling day. There were white moonflowers which emerged only at night slowly easing their delicate petals open, while the myriad birds sang exultantly.

Conceição was waiting on the porch as Tony arrived, and he gave her a kiss before going inside to pick up his Smith & Wesson. After more than a hundred practice rounds, he'd become quite a proficient gunslinger but was still not entirely comfortable with the notion of wearing the gun all the time.

That night, after a dinner of beefy and pasta, they made languid love and fell into a fitful sleep. In the early hours of the morning, though, Tony awoke in a trembling sweat, shivering uncontrollably and with a throbbing headache: malaria aftershock.

For the next three days he lay cursing out loud and quietly pleading, in the grip of fever, eyes burning huge in his sallow face, Conceição feeding him warm broths made of shreds of chicken and jungle herbs. The nights were the worst, when his insides seemed to be boiling and his skin was clammy with cold sweat, until the early hours, when he would fall into a slumber brought on by exhaustion.

On the fourth morning, once the fever had broken again and he slept deeply under a cool fan, he had a dream. He was alone, stripped to the waist, cotton trousers rolled up and his hair floating in the breeze as he made his way cautiously across a precarious rope bridge slung across a ravine. He was halfway across, suspended between two walls of green above an abyss from which, far below, came the sound of rushing water, when he noticed a faint smell of smoke. He swung around, the bridge wobbling dangerously, and saw a tongue of flame snaking its way along the rope behind him. He tried to run, but his movements were agonisingly slow, his legs dead weights and his breath coming in short, sharp, painful stabs. Somewhere he could hear a voice singing: 'O-Hay nya, ititnakatdyer, O-Hay nya, ititnakatdyer, murra, taka, hopi, sou na!' It was, he realised, Pitanga!

He woke up with a jolt, bathed in sweat. The first thing that struck him was that the smell of smoke was still with him, pricking at his nostrils and growing stronger. Excited cries rent the pre-dawn air, and despite the time a bright glow lit up the sky.

He scrambled out of bed, Conceição following, and ran outside, where he gaped in disbelief at the fire raging in the jungle, in the direction of the waterfall. It was too far away to be certain, but he knew inside himself that he was not mistaken, and his heart sank. The unthinkable had happened. *Was* happening!

He ran to Roberto's bungalow and shook his friend violently. 'Wake up! Hurry! There's a fire!'

Roberto was immediately awake and pulling on a pair of trousers, stepping into hide boots, while Raimunda looked on uncomprehendingly with sleep-filled eyes. 'Where's the fire?' Roberto demanded.

'I'm not one hundred percent sure, but it looks like around the waterfall.'

'That bastard de Brito! I'd slit his throat and pull his tongue out through the hole!' Raimunda suddenly spat out. Tony looked at her in astonishment. 'Now is the time when you must stand by Roberto; he needs your help,' she told him.

'Let's go,' Roberto cut in, rifle in one hand and ready to move. 'You have your gun?'

Tony hesitated. 'Er, shit, no.'

'Go get it and follow the rest of us.'

Soon he was running after Roberto, Lourenco, Pitanga and a couple of the other farmhands along the path to the waterfall. It was so hot the air itself seemed to be on fire, burning the lungs. They hacked branches from trees to beat the flames, but as they raced into the clearing, they each knew without saying that their task was a futile one. The fire was burning freely on three sides of the pool, the placid water reflecting the blaze in a ghostly glare, and there was a strong smell of petrol in the air.

Roberto let out a piercing howl and flung himself desperately at the nearest flames, beating furiously. The others joined without protest, even if they knew it was hopeless. They beat with the energy of madmen, but no sooner would they smother one group of flames than another seemed to spring up. The thick smoke caught in their throats, choking them, and stung their eyes. Soon they were all coated in black ash, but they worked without rest until it was already dawn and their branches were blackened sticks, the leaves burnt away.

Feeble sunlight filtered through the smoke, thin spirals still rising all around from the scorched earth. The world was grey, and the group of men retreated to where the forest was untouched and slumped to the ground in defeat. Somehow, through superhuman effort, they had managed to kill the flames, but what had been their private paradise had been razed to the ground, scarred black. The soil felt warm underneath them, and clumps of undergrowth smouldered on.

'It'll grow back,' Tony muttered, wiping sweat from his brow.

'It will, but not the same,' Roberto growled. 'Those sons of bitches, I'm going to kill them this time. They will never drive me out.'

'You want to go there now? I'm coming with you, then.'

'No, you mustn't. This is my fight, not yours.'

'Oh, fuck off,' Tony told him. 'We're in this together. If we're going to do it, let's just do it.'

CHAPTER THIRTEEN

A Reckoning

They walked in sullen silence back through the clamorous, frightened forest. At Water Flower Garden, they washed and accepted coffee from Conceição and Raimunda, and checked their weapons.

'Okay, let's do it,' Roberto said at last, and rose to his feet. He and Tony clambered into the red Ford truck, and Lourenco joined them in the back with an old shotgun.

They drove slowly across the red dirt highway to the gates of Rio Novo, and stopped. Francisco barred the way, standing hands on hips, a smirk on his face, on each side of him a farmhand. All were carrying machetes, and Francisco had a hand over his holstered pistol.

'Where's fucking de Brito?' Roberto snarled at him.

'What's it got to do with you?' Francisco sneered back.

'You know very well what it has got to do with me. The fire. You bastards set the fucking fire on my land!' Roberto was seething but kept his voice under control.

'I don't know what you are talking about. Now I suggest you get off Mr de Brito's land.' Francisco turned away and began moving back towards the farmhouse.

Roberto opened his door and climbed out. 'Not so fast!' he shouted, then he suddenly fired a shot into the air.

Francisco ducked and whirled around, went down on one knee and loosed off a shot of his own, missing everyone, even the car. He dived into the thick undergrowth on the side of the driveway. The two farmhands who'd been with him ran off back towards the house, shouting.

'I think we better leave the truck here,' Roberto said. 'If we drive in, we'll be sitting ducks. Let's fan out.'

'I'm going to circle around in the forest to look for Francisco,' Tony answered. 'Just be careful; there might be others.'

He pushed aside some shrubs and entered the strip of jungle that had been left untouched either side of the driveway. He walked slowly and carefully, putting into practice all the skills he'd learned about moving silently through the forest. Fortunately for him, Francisco was a city man, and less experienced in jungle craft – and he'd made the classic mistake of lighting a cigarette. Tony could smell the smoke long before he spotted de Brito's enforcer; he was crouched behind a bush where the edge of the vegetation ran alongside the driveway, aiming his pistol at Roberto, who was advancing cautiously, Lourenco slightly behind him on the other side of the path.

'I wouldn't do that if I were you.' Tony warned in his deep voice.

Francisco spun around and shot wildly, the bullet embedding itself in a thick tree several yards from its target. Tony didn't think twice; he let off two shots of his own in quick succession, and saw the Brazilian throw his arms up as he fell back and dropped his gun, swearing loudly. Tony quickly advanced and scooped up the fallen weapon, keeping his own trained on the stricken Francisco. He wasn't dead, but he was in a lot of pain and bleeding profusely from a large hole in his right shoulder. The other bullet must have missed.

'Filho de puta,' Francisco groaned through gritted teeth. 'I'm going to kill you.'

'I don't think so; not this time, amigo,' Tony told him. 'Now get up.'

Roberto joined them, while Lourenco stayed on the driveway, watching all around. 'Good hunting. One down; bring him with us!'

Francisco struggled to his feet while Tony kept his gun levelled, tucking the spare pistol into the back of his slacks.

Back on the driveway, Roberto pushed Francisco in front of him, jabbing him in the back with the barrel of his Winchester copy.

Tony opened his Smith & Wesson and filled the two empty chambers of the drum. Then they moved slowly forwards again, until the dark house came into view.

De Brito was on the veranda, in his hands the unmistakeable silhouette of an Uzi machine pistol, one of the most recognisable guns in the world. In the right hands it was deadly in close combat. In inexperienced hands, it could be wildly inaccurate, spraying its thirty-two rounds in a haphazard arc, but that was little comfort.

They stopped some fifty yards from the building, looking all around, wondering if de Brito was alone or if there were others hidden from view. The place reeked of hidden menace, but nothing stirred. There was no sign of life, other than a rat-like dog lying in the dust, dozing with its bloodshot eyes half open. The only sound was Francisco's ragged breathing.

'What are you doing on my land?' de Brito shouted at them. 'What have you done to Francisco? You will pay for this.'

'We came to see you about the fire. We know it was you!' Roberto shouted back. 'Francisco shot at us first. He was hit when we fired back, it was self-defence, so the only one who is going to pay is you, you whoreson!'

'I know nothing about a fire; now get off my land. I'm going to the police, or maybe the military, yes, even better. I know people.'

'You and your dog Francisco here were seen at the scene of the fire,' Roberto lied. 'We have proof.'

Without warning, de Brito squeezed the trigger of his Uzi, spraying bullets. Francisco was hit several times, which saved Roberto, even though he was also hit, twice in one of his legs, as the other man slumped forwards.

De Brito rushed to put a new magazine into his weapon, and there were suddenly two almighty bangs as Lourenco loosed off both barrels of his old shotgun, the blast of pellets taking de Brito straight in the face. He dropped the Uzi and fell to his knees, hands covering his eyes. 'I can't see! I can't see!' he wailed.

Roberto limped forwards, his left leg drenched in blood, and stood over de Brito. 'Who else is here?'

'No one, no one, I sent them all away,' de Brito sobbed. 'I need a hospital, help me!'

'You need a morgue,' Roberto told him, then raised his rifle and shot de Brito through the head from point-blank range.

'What the fuck?' Tony ran forwards. 'You murdered him!'

'I didn't have a choice, my friend; it was kill or be killed. That is the way here. Now help me.' Roberto spoke softly, his mood sombre.

Together with Lourenco they dragged Francisco and de Brito's bodies inside the house. Using a half-full jerry can they found in an adjacent barn, they splashed petrol liberally inside and out. Then Roberto threw a lighted match and the building erupted into flames.

'We were lucky he was alone,' Roberto said as they retreated back to the car. 'Maybe he just expected us to roll over; he was used to always getting his way. He was too arrogant and got careless.' Roberto was also lucky in that his wounds were just flesh wounds; no bullets had stayed in his leg, and no vital arteries had been hit.

Tony shook his head. 'I still can't believe that happened. I shot a man! You killed de Brito, and now you've set fire to his house. And what are you doing with the Uzi?'

'The fire will destroy the evidence. They may work out that they were shot, but not by who.' Roberto gestured with the Uzi in his hands. 'And this I will keep, safely hidden away. You need to give me Francisco's pistol as well. And you should leave, at least for a while.'

Back at Water Flower Garden they washed and burned their old clothes. Once Raimunda had dressed his wounds, Roberto hid the guns.

Despite the barrage of questions thrown at them by Conceição and Raimunda, Roberto and Tony remained tight-lipped. 'There was an accident; it's all over now,' was all Roberto would say. In time they would learn the truth, but now was not that time; there were still things to be done. Not least, Tony had a decision to make.

CHAPTER FOURTEEN

A Departure

'Why do you think I should leave?' Tony asked Roberto as they sat together in their usual place on the veranda, bottle of pinga between them. He was still shaken by the events earlier, still couldn't believe that their small piece of paradise had been blown apart. 'I thought you said the cops would never be able to join the dots.'

'I don't think they will.' Roberto sighed. 'But the fact is, de Brito was a powerful man with a lot of connections. They might come poking around; I can handle that, but they could make life very uncomfortable for you. I just think you need to lie low. Leave the country for the time being, maybe go to Bolivia until everything cools down. It's not far; you can cross the river. Pitanga can go with you as a guide.'

'This river here in Porto Velho? The Madeira?'

'Yes. You take the road for a bit, to get around the waterfalls, until you get to the junction of the Mamoré and Beni rivers at Villa Bella. That's pretty much the Bolivian border, across the other side of the river. There's a crossing point at Guajará-Mirim on the Mamoré River.'

'Why don't I just fly? Go to La Paz, maybe?'

'I think better to avoid the airport. By land is less conspicuous.'

'Fuck.' Tony knocked back his glass of pinga and sucked on a lemon, feeling devastated. 'I feel at home here. And what about Conceição?'

Roberto spread his hands helplessly. 'She can stay here as long as she wants, look after the house, until you come back.'

'Maybe she'd want to come with me? But I don't know if she

even has a passport.'

'Probably not. And there's no time to get one. I think you should prepare to leave tomorrow, the quicker the better, before the authorities come nosing around.'

Roberto was right; Conceição didn't have a passport, and she was distraught when Tony told her he was leaving. 'What will happen to me?' she asked, tears streaming down her face.

'I'll come back. Or you can join me; I'll leave you money, but you need to get a passport,' Tony answered as he slung his few belongings into his leather bag.

That night they made frenzied love, as if it were the end of their world, which in a way it was. Neither knew it then, but after the morning they would never see each other again.

*

Pitanga was waiting outside the house with a shy smile on his Asiatic face as dawn broke. Tony showered and ate some scrambled eggs that Conceição had prepared, washed down with the usual sweet black coffee. Then Roberto drove them all to the bus station in Porto Velho.

Shortly afterwards, and after more tears from Conceição, Tony went to board the bus for the five-and-a-half hours' ride to Guajará-Mirim. 'I'll write to you at the poste restante,' he told Conceição and Roberto. 'Don't forget to check for mail.'

'Até logo, amigo. I'll see you soon.' Roberto shook Tony's hand, and then pulled him in for a bear hug. Then Tony and Pitanga climbed aboard, where they found seats near to the front, and soon afterwards they disappeared in a cloud of dust.

The road, such as it was, followed the corridor of the old railway. Tony remembered Roberto had told him that in what seemed like another lifetime. He stared out of the window, not talking, as they passed the first of the nineteen waterfalls that the railway had been built to circumvent. Then he turned to Pitanga. 'You didn't have to come, you know. I could manage on my own. But I'm grateful.'

The small man shrugged. 'I am happy. After you cross the river, I will go and visit my tribe.'

'Where do they live?'

'We have a reservation, a big one. It's on the way to Guajará-Mirim.'

'How many are in your tribe?' Tony thought the man looked as if he could be Southeast Asian. He wondered where these Indians had originally come from and how they'd arrived in the Amazon forest, or if they'd always been here.

'Not so many, a few hundred, much less than a thousand. Most of us have very little contact with the white man's world, and we like it that way. That's why I can't take you there; the chief wouldn't like it.'

Tony was intrigued. 'How do you live? Do the Karitiana have farms?'

'Not really, not like the white man. We live with the forest. I mean, we farm a few things in small fields, but otherwise we fish and we hunt. We are happy with our ways of doing things; we don't want to be like the white man.'

They lapsed into silence again, watching the jungle fly past, the river never far away as they followed the old railway route past the waterfalls, until they reached the junction of the Madeira and the Mamoré rivers and turned towards Guajará-Mirim.

From the bus station, Pitanga walked with Tony down to the riverside, where he could catch a boat over to Guayaramerín on the Bolivian side. Tony shook his hand, the Indian's hand surprisingly soft, then Pitanga turned and walked away without a backwards glance.

Once in Guayaramerín, Tony passed through the ramshackle customs hut and, for a modest fee, collected an entry stamp in his passport. He found a simple but clean hostel for the night, and went in search of some food while he pondered his next move. He thought he'd go to La Paz eventually, but he wasn't ready to face a large city so quickly after his time at Water Flower Garden. He needed some breathing space in between.

He wondered how long he'd need to be away. He felt desperate and lost; he was running away but had no idea where to, as if he'd been cast adrift and his life had lost all meaning again. He'd found paradise, and it had been snatched away from him, and he had no idea how he would replace that in his life.

That evening, as he sat in a restaurant enjoying a plate of fish and rice, he noticed one of his neighbours had a Lonely Planet guide on his table, and asked if he could have a look at it. The other traveller, an American by the looks of him, obliged, and told Tony to take his time as he was still waiting for his meal.

Tony leafed through the book's section on Bolivia, and found himself settling on a place called Rurrenabaque on the River Beni in the north of the country, right at the edge of the Madidi National Park. It was a centre for eco-tourism and described as Bolivia's 'gateway to the Amazon', and Tony thought it sounded like the ideal place to while away a few days while he thought about his next move. Especially as Guayaramerín itself clearly had little to offer.

CHAPTER FIFTEEN

Rurre

Early the following morning, Tony embarked on another excruciating bone-shaking eleven-hour bus ride, scrunched into another child-sized seat next to a large indigenous woman with a bowler hat. Judging by the smell, Tony reckoned it must have been several weeks since she'd had a proper wash, but with the help of some sleeping tablets he'd picked up in Guayaramerín he survived the mind-numbing jolting and the heat.

He arrived in Rurrenabaque in the early evening and booked into the grandly named Hotel Oriental in the Plaza 2 de Febrero, which also hosted the town hall, a church, and a small naval base. Tony was amused to find out in the next few days that every morning a naval cadet blew tunelessly on a trumpet as the Bolivian flag was raised. He guessed that, in a country without any sea, the navy just had to make do as best it could with what it did have: the rivers and half of Lake Titicaca.

The Hotel Oriental was basic but clean, with a charming inner courtyard full of hammocks, where guests could laze away the hot afternoons, reading or just snoozing. The hotel also provided a perfectly adequate breakfast of fruit, boiled eggs, fresh bread rolls and coffee, and Tony felt he'd chosen well.

He soon discovered that Rurrenabaque, or 'Rurre', as the locals called it, was a vibrant town with plenty of shops and small restaurants and even a couple of swimming pools in the more upmarket hotels, which anyone could visit for a small fee. Tourism was in its infancy, but there were a couple of agents offering jungle walks and a visit to the nearby wetlands of the pampas on the Yacuma River.

Tony felt he'd already done his fair share of jungle walking, so he opted for a three-day outing to the pampas instead. But first he wrote letters to Roberto and Conceição via the poste restante in Porto Velho, letting them know he was fine and thinking of heading to La Paz within the week, so they should send any replies there, and asking after their news.

After a three-hour drive along a dirt road – Tony wondered if there were *any* asphalted roads in Bolivia – they arrived at the lodge in Santa Rosa de Yacuma. It was basic but adequate, and at least the rough wooden beds were covered with mosquito netting. The pampas were open wetlands, and for the following two days he sat in a motorised canoe and watched a bewildering display of wildlife float by: huge capybaras which looked like giant rats, kingfishers, blue and yellow macaws, turtles, capuchin monkeys, black caimans, an anaconda, and, best of all, pods of pink river dolphins.

The guide said it was fine to swim with the dolphins, but, bearing in mind the anacondas, alligators and piranhas, Tony thought it wiser to decline the offer. They did, however, catch half a dozen piranhas on the first day, which they took back with them to be cooked for their evening meal. It was a bony fish and a lot of work to eat, not something Tony felt he would acquire a taste for. Give him a Dover sole any day.

Back in Rurre, he spent another few days just relaxing, mostly in a hammock in the courtyard of the Hotel Oriental or shopping for trinkets, steeling himself for the 'road of death' to La Paz.

The Yungas Road to the capital was notorious; literally hundreds of vehicles dropped off the unprotected edges every year, killing around one hundred people. In parts it was only three or four yards wide, and Tony had his heart in his mouth as the bus slid around corners. He was grateful at least that they were climbing, which restricted their speed. The other direction, going downhill, would surely have been far worse. But eight hours into the journey, the way was blocked by a rockfall, and there was nothing to do but join a queue of other vehicles and wait another six hours until the road was cleared.

They finally hit a stretch of blissful asphalt and crawled into La Paz, past jerry-built houses in dusty streets and a large metallic statue of Che Guevara, some twenty hours after they'd set out.

CHAPTER SIXTEEN

La Paz

Although the climb to La Paz, some 12,000 feet above sea level and the highest capital city in the world, had been slow, Tony immediately felt out of breath from altitude sickness, which he knew would take two or three days to become accustomed to. He checked into a simple guest house near the Witches' Market in the centre of the city, and went to take a shower, which was cold. Hot water was among many items in short supply in La Paz.

He decided to stay in the city until he had word from Water Flower Garden, however long it took. But it was uncomfortable; he was constantly cold, and not having hot water didn't help, although the altitude sickness eased after three days.

The Witches' Market kept him busy for a couple of days, wandering through a maze of tents and shops specialising in the sale of traditional medicines, including dried frogs and armadillos, and llama foetuses, the last apparently promising good fortune to the purchaser, although Tony decided to give them a miss. He was, however, careful to be on his best behaviour in these shops, in case he ended up having to deal with a curse of some kind.

On the third day he went to the central post office to check if there was any mail, dodging around a demonstration of striking tin miners who were throwing sticks of dynamite about in the streets. The traffic was relatively light, but the exhaust fumes sat low in the thin air and, with the smoke from the dynamite added to them, Tony found himself gasping for breath again. Unfortunately, the effort was wasted, as there was no mail.

In the following days he continued to explore the city on foot, but there was little to get excited about. Perhaps the only area he enjoyed was the old colonial area of Calle Jaén, with its cobblestone streets, colourful houses, several museums, and plenty of restaurants and bars he could drop into. There was also the Basilica of San Francisco, dating back to the eighteenth century, but you could only spend so much time in a church. One day he also spent an hour trekking around the so-called Valley of the Moon some six miles outside La Paz, where the erosion of the mountains had formed tall spires of clay and sandstone. Apparently, it got its name after a visit by the American astronaut Neil Armstrong, who'd said it looked like the moon to him.

Finally, after he'd been in La Paz for ten days, Tony found a letter waiting for him at the poste restante, but it was not good news. Roberto wrote that he had been briefly detained after the police had come to inspect the ruins of Rio Novo. It seemed that the two farm workers who had been with Francisco and had run off had reported that Roberto had arrived at the farm with a gun, along with a gringo who was also armed. However, Roberto didn't believe they could make any charges against him stick, and he expected to be in the clear once the police had run out of ideas.

To make matters worse, Conceição had gone off on her own, apparently to Brasília, in search of a passport. That was what she had told Raimunda, but Roberto worried that she might find it difficult in the big city and said he should have gone with her. He advised Tony to stay away, and said once things had died down, he'd probably return to his home state of Rio Grande do Sul. Tony had his mother's address and could write to him there.

Back at his guest house, Tony read the letter again, and then again. 'Fuck, fuck, and fuck again,' he muttered. 'It's all gone to dogshit.'

He lay back on his bed and stared at the ceiling, wondering what to do. He knew he couldn't stay in Bolivia; there didn't seem much point. It was cold and dirty, the food was poor, and he wanted a hot shower.

He considered his options: go back to England, continue to travel in South America, or try somewhere completely different – New

Zealand or Australia, perhaps. There were flights across the Pacific. Once again, his life seemed to have no purpose.

As ever, fate intervened and made the decision for him. That evening he decided to try to cheer himself up by visiting one of the city's best hotels for a proper steak meal and a decent bottle of wine. He endured another cold shower and managed to shave, put on a clean set of clothes, and headed off to the Ritz Hotel in the Plaza Isabel la Católica in the city centre.

Enjoying a gin vermouth in the hotel's bar before venturing into Duke's Restaurant, he struck up a conversation with a small man about his own age.

'My name is Bill,' the man introduced himself in a thick Spanish accent. He had jet black hair swept back, a cheeky smile and sparkling eyes so dark they could almost have been black. 'You are a gringo, yes?'

Tony sighed. *Here we go again,* he thought. 'No, I'm English, as it happens.'

'Ah, Inglés, now that is different. I love England; I've been to London a few times. Yes, I have friends there.'

'Seriously? On holiday?'

'On holiday, yes, and some business.'

'What kind of business?'

'Oh, this and that.'

'And how did you get a name like Bill? Doesn't sound very Bolivian to me.'

'Actually, my real name is Guillermo, which, as you probably know, is Spanish for William, but my friends call me Bill. For me, it's like a disguise, you know. And I'm not Bolivian, I'm from Colombia.'

'Colombia?' Tony was intrigued. 'What are you doing here, then? Another holiday?'

'And some business, maybe. In fact, my father is the ambassador here.'

'Wow! Are you staying in this hotel?'

'Just for a couple of nights, then I go home to Bogotá. What about you?'

'Ah, no, this place is a bit too grand for me, I just came for a meal. But can I offer you another drink?'

Bill accepted and ordered a singani, a local brandy made from muscat of Alexandria grapes. 'So, tell me, Inglés, what are *you* doing here? For business as well?'

'It's a long story,' Tony said. He went on to tell his companion some of his experiences in Rondônia, and, without going into specifics, gave a rough idea of why he had to leave.

'Quite a tale,' Bill said at the end. 'So, what now?'

'I really don't know. Can't really stay here; there's nothing for me in Bolivia. Maybe I'll go home, or maybe somewhere else. Now, though, I'm going to eat. I hope the steaks are good here.'

'Oh, they are, amigo. But I tell you what: if you go north, come and visit me in Bogotá.' And he gave Tony his card. 'Maybe we can do some business?'

Tony looked at the card. 'Hmm. Bogotá, Colombia, eh? Heard it can be a bit of a rough place, dangerous.'

'All places can be dangerous. For example, el sur de la ciudad, the south of the city, is very dangerous, very poor. But the north, where the rich people live, is beautiful; you can have a lot of fun there. And Colombia is a very beautiful country. There are a lot of clever people there. I am sure the first king of the world will be a Colombian,' he said with a laugh.

'I'll think about it, thank you,' Tony said, as he got up to leave and they shook hands.

'Be sure that you do; you will be very welcome!'

The steak was as good as promised, and as Tony worked his way through it, and a bottle of fine Chilean cabernet sauvignon, he thought about the offer. He wondered what kind of business 'Bill' was in; he'd certainly been very cagey about it. But then what did he have to lose?

The next morning, he came to a decision. He would go to Bogotá. But while he was in South America, it felt a shame not to see some of its attractions on the way, so he would go first to Lake Titicaca, which was only a three-hour bus ride, cross into Peru, and make his way up to Cuzco. From there he could take a train to Aguas Calientes to see the wonders of Machu Picchu.

Machu Picchu turned out to be one of those gobsmackingly astonishing manmade places that exceed anything you could possibly imagine, like, for example, the Great Wall of China, or the giant Buddhas of Bamiyan in Afghanistan if you were lucky enough to have seen them before the Taliban blew them up.

Tony rose well before dawn to make the two-hour trek up the mountain, so he was at the Sun Gate to see the sunrise, and then enjoyed several hours almost by himself in the Inca city, wondering how on earth they had managed to build such structures without cement, all dry-stone walls. Probably used plenty of slaves, but still. He was still lost in wonder when the first of the tourist buses started arriving at about ten o'clock, and decided it was time to leave.

Back in Cuzco, he caught a flight to Lima, and put in a call to Bill. Was he really serious about visiting him in Bogotá? Tony was assured that the offer was entirely serious, he'd be met at the airport, just send the flight details.

So it was that, two days later, Tony found himself aboard an Avianca flight and making the steep descent into El Dorado airport. Before leaving Peru, he'd sent another letter to Roberto, via his mother's address, advising him of his movements and asking after further news of Water Flower Garden, and if Conceição had reappeared.

CHAPTER SEVENTEEN

Bogotá

Tony cleared immigration and customs with the minimum of fuss, and was relieved when he saw that Bill, true to his word, was waiting on the other side. Tony had been wondering what his next move would be if no one turned up to meet him, as he didn't really have an alternative plan.

'Welcome to Bogotá!' Bill grinned. 'Come, tonight you can stay at our house, then maybe tomorrow we can go to my farm; it's not far out of the city. Can you ride?'

'Horses or motorbikes?'

'Horses, of course; you'd be mad to get on a motorbike here.'

'Well, I can, but badly.'

'You'll be fine. Maybe we'll try shooting some skeet.' He took Tony's bag, and they headed outside to where an attendant was guarding his Renault. 'This is all you got?'

'Yes, that's it, I'm afraid.'

The evening air was cool, and again Tony felt slightly out of breath from the altitude. At a little under 9,000 feet, Bogotá wasn't a whole lot lower than La Paz. It was a long, thin city nestling in a valley beneath high mountain peaks, mostly laid out in grid form with the carreras (avenues) running north to south, intersected by the calles (streets) running east to west, and the traffic was anarchic. The higher the number of the calle, the further north it was.

Bill guided them up to La Septima, carrera number seven, and then headed north until he reached Calle 146, a small street high above the city, whose lights twinkled into the far distance below. The street, just north of Usaquén Park, was tidy, and the houses were all different but looked spacious and well kept, though Tony noticed that all the cars were kept behind locked gates, and the house windows had bars on them.

At Bill's house they were greeted by his wife Isobel, a slim auburn-haired woman with hazel eyes and a ready smile, and his two children, an eight-year-old daughter called Pilar and two-year-old son Juan. A roast chicken dinner was ready, and the maid set an extra place for their visitor.

They made small talk while they ate the food, mostly questions about Tony's travels and what his plans were – the latter of which he had no real answer for. He just felt he was travelling with no idea of his destination, as if he were running from somewhere without knowing where he was running to. He also realised he'd need to work on his Spanish if he was going to spend any real length of time in Colombia.

Once dinner ended, Bill announced that they were going out for 'postre', dessert, while the kids got ready for bed. They drove further up the mountain for about ten minutes, and stopped outside a small bar. Inside, Tony discovered they were the only ones there, apart from a couple of other friends of Bill and Isobel's, introduced as Carlos and Pablo. 'Carlos Lehder and Pablo Escobar,' Bill joked.

It was indeed the era of the cartels, with Carlos Lehder and Pablo Escobar being the co-founders of the notorious Medellín cartel. They were part of the reason Tony had felt Colombia might be a dangerous place to visit, given that it was known as the murder capital of the world. Escobar was ultimately blamed for the deaths of some 4,000 people, although some saw him as a sort of modern-day Robin Hood after he spent millions on some of Medellín's poorest neighbourhoods, building houses, parks, football stadiums, hospitals, schools and churches. But then he could afford it, given that his cartel controlled around eighty percent of the cocaine trafficked into North America, earning him approximately $420 million a week.

A bottle of aguardiente, the popular Colombian alcohol with an anise base, was placed on the table, along with glasses and, curiously, a saucer and a teaspoon.

'What's with the saucer?' Tony asked as Bill poured him a shot of the aguardiente.

'That's for the dessert, of course,' Bill replied as the others laughed. Carlos produced a plastic bag of white powder, which he emptied into the saucer.

'Is that what I think it is?'

'The famous White Lady, my friend. Colombia's greatest export. Along with coffee, flowers, emeralds and oil, to be fair.' Bill picked up the teaspoon, scooped up what looked like half a gram of the cocaine, sprinkled it onto his hand between the thumb and forefinger, and then snorted the lot, a fair amount spilling down his front.

'I thought you were supposed to chop it up and use a rolled bank note or something,' Tony observed. 'That seems quite wasteful.'

'At a dollar a gram it doesn't really matter,' Carlos replied. 'Here, try some.'

'I've never tried cocaine before,' Tony told him, copying Bill's actions.

'Seriously? You'll love it, and it's pure, not all cut up and mixed with other stuff like in the US or Europe.'

Tony sniffed cautiously at first, then ingested everything on his hand. The effect was instantaneous, a rush of heightened awareness and a numbing in his throat. He licked off the few bits that remained on his hand, and felt his tongue and gums go numb as well, as the saucer was passed around the table. 'Wow, I feel so full of energy all of a sudden, on top of the world!'

They sat there until the wee hours, drinking two bottles of aguardiente, smoking a lot of cigarettes, and talking endlessly about stuff they probably wouldn't remember the next day. At one point Tony asked Bill about his business.

'Import–export, mostly,' came the reply, with one of his cheeky grins.

'Importing and exporting what, exactly?' Tony was starting to feel a bit on edge and had begun grinding his teeth.

'Flowers to London and Rotterdam, mostly, then we import money back.' Everyone thought that was very funny.

'Nothing to do with this stuff, then?' Tony nodded at the near-empty saucer.

'Been thinking about it, to be honest. There's a lot of money in it, and it's quite easy. I just need some safe addresses in the US and Europe, and people who can handle it.'

'Isn't it dangerous? What about the cartels? What if you step on their toes?'

'We wouldn't. There's such a feast going on at the top table that there are plenty of crumbs for the little people. We wouldn't need to stick our heads above the parapet, just keep it small and a low profile, and there's not much that can go wrong.'

*

Unsurprisingly, Tony found it hard to sleep that night, but he awoke early anyway to find the house was quiet, and he realised it was a Saturday. Only the maid was up, and she brought him coffee and pastries. The others appeared in ones and twos over the next couple of hours, and before midday they were in the car on their way to Bill's farm in La Calera, about forty minutes north of the city.

As promised, Bill asked for a couple of horses to be saddled up and they set off riding. Isobel and the children stayed behind to prepare churrasco, grilled steaks over an open fire with a homemade chimichurri marinade: an Argentinian speciality made with fresh parsley, oregano, garlic, olive oil, vinegar and red pepper.

The sky was a moody grey, threatening rain, and Tony wore a pullover against the cool mountain air. He and Bill both carried rifles.

'You really think we'll find some game?' Tony asked.

'Like I said, we'll try to flush out some skeet. But they're hard to shoot, very fast, and small.'

They headed towards a small copse and waited while a couple of the farm workers entered the woods to act as beaters. Tony and Bill sat on their horses, rifles at the ready, listening to the whoops and yells of the farmhands, until suddenly three birds flashed out into the open, flying low. They both fired. Tony's horse bolted and he tumbled from the saddle, getting up with a grin as Bill burst into laughter.

'Fuck, lucky we didn't kill each other there!' Tony said.

'I got one!' Bill announced, as one of the beaters ran up with a tiny mangled corpse.

'You did? Christ, they were impossible to hit. What are you going to do with it?'

'Eat it. A hunter must always eat his food.'

'That wouldn't fill up an Ethiopian!'

'You're right, but it's the principle; you can't shoot things just for fun. Come, we can go back now and see how lunch is progressing.'

'What's for dessert?'

'Ha! You are catching on, my friend!'

The churrasco was delicious, and along with the meat there were tiny, very yellow sweet potatoes. 'These are amazing; never seen potatoes like these before,' Tony remarked.

'They are papas criolla from Colombia,' Isobel told him. 'You know we have literally thousands of different kinds of potatoes in South America; Peru probably has the most. But most are not suitable for export, maybe because they don't keep for long once you have dug them up. This is where potatoes came from.'

'Yes, I did know that. And that when they first arrived in Europe, they were banned in Scotland because they aren't mentioned in the Bible.'

'Is that true? That's really funny,' Bill said.

Afterwards Tony spent some time playing draughts with Pilar, allowing her to win. In the evening, they sat around a fire indoors, sampling some more of Bill's 'postre' with a couple of whiskies, but were much more restrained than the previous evening.

'So how do you like Colombia so far?' Isobel asked.

'Well, it's nothing like I expected so far, that's for sure,' Tony replied. 'After we go back to Bogotá, I think I'm going to go out into the country for a couple of weeks, learn the language and think about what we talked about.'

'Learn the language in the country? What do you mean?'

'Well, I figured I'd go somewhere fairly remote, where no one speaks English, and that way I'd have to learn Spanish. And I have a dictionary, so I can learn fifty or a hundred or so words a day.'

Isobel laughed and clapped her hands. 'It's certainly original. Let's think of a good place to go, then. I'll help you.'

CHAPTER EIGHTEEN

Tierradentro

Isobel decided that Tierradentro, meaning 'inside earth', would be a good choice. It was located in Cauca, in the southwest of Colombia. 'The thing is, it's one of the most important archaeological sites in South America and it's supposed to be really beautiful, but nobody has ever heard of it. Hardly any tourists go there, there are no big towns, and I doubt if anyone speaks English.'

'Sounds good to me, but it's a long way away, isn't it? How would I get there? Don't tell me by bus; I've kind of had my fill of buses lately.'

'Fly to Popayán; it's a nice city. Spend a night or two there, then take the bus. It should only be four or five hours from there, maybe less.'

Tony had his doubts, but everywhere else they looked, from Cartagena on the Caribbean coast to Medellín or Cali or even Los Llanos in the east, would likely be teeming with tourists, guerrillas or drug traffickers, so in the end he agreed that Tierradentro it would be.

First, though, he made a trip to the centre of Bogotá to visit the poste restante; there was no letter, so he sent another to Roberto, giving him Bill's address and saying he would be back in a couple of weeks. He then spent the rest of the day wandering around the historic old centre of the city, La Candelaria, with its bohemian streets and cafés and colourful houses in red, white, blue and green. He visited the gold museum, which was rammed with artifacts from the pre-Hispanic cultures, masks, bowls, jewellery, armour and more, and finished off by taking the funicular railway to Monserrate, a hill which towered over Bogotá and offered a breathtaking panoramic view of the city.

The next day he flew to Popayán with Avianca. He was slightly perturbed to discover the aircraft was a twin-propeller wooden-hulled affair, but the mountain views were spectacular, and the ninety minutes the journey took were without doubt an improvement on the twelve hours or more of discomfort that the bus offered on poor roads.

And Popayán was indeed a beautiful city, full of colonial architecture, the buildings mostly white, and a foodie's paradise. The empanadas he bought were probably the best Tony had ever tasted, and that evening he enjoyed half a spit-roast chicken with spicy aji sauce, which was also spectacular. Unbeknownst to him, the city would be devastated by a huge earthquake less than a year later, in March 1983.

He booked into a hotel near the bus terminal after discovering there was a bus to San Andrés de Pisimbalá in Tierradentro at ten the next morning, and went to bed excited by the prospect of his forthcoming adventure.

The bus turned out to be a chiva, that unique Colombian invention where the open-sided chassis was made from brightly painted wood, usually with a Dodge or a Ford engine at the front, a flat roof for cargo, and rows of seats inside that ran the whole width of the vehicle, seating six or seven people. They were tough and designed for narrow, winding roads, perfect for the needs of the campesinos carrying their goods to market or to town, and they had no doors. Each row of seats could be entered either side of the vehicle through a space in the chassis, and Tony made sure to grab himself a seat at one end of a row.

It was uncomfortable, but he found himself enjoying himself with the friendly crowd around him. Sure enough, none spoke English, but, with signs and using his Brazilian Portuguese, he managed to make himself understood for the most part. In any case, the language barriers didn't stop the other passengers from bombarding him with questions and offering him a selection of fruits, empanadas and tamales during the five-hour journey.

Eventually he was dropped off at a lane which led the last mile or so to the village of San Andrés de Pisimbalá. It was little more than a collection of half a dozen small houses and a store selling basic essentials, but he found a room easily enough with one of the local families and spent the next couple of days exploring his new surroundings, content that there seemed to be no other tourists around.

The lack of tourists astonished him as he wandered around the hillsides, discovering numerous pre-Hispanic tombs dotted around, sometimes eight or even ten yards deep underground and twelve or fifteen yards wide. The walls were still covered with faded black and red geometric patterns, which he later found out were believed to date back to 600 or 900 AD. No one seemed sure who had built them. It wasn't believed to be the Páez Indians, who still inhabited the surrounding mountains in their tens of thousands.

Standing inside the tombs, in the silence, Tony was sure he could feel a *presence*, without knowing how to describe it. It was, however, deeply spiritual.

The local Páez Indians were believed to be one of the few indigenous tribes never to have been completely defeated by the Spanish, even as they were pushed further and further up into the mountains. They were still persecuted, both by guerrillas and by paramilitaries, but they clung stubbornly to their old beliefs, even if their shamanism now had some Catholic influences. Most spoke only Páez, a language related to Chibcha.

After several days walking around on his own, building up his Spanish vocabulary, Tony decided he wanted to find out more about the Páez, and, after meeting a local farm worker who was half Indian and spoke the language, he persuaded him to act as his guide for a hike across the mountains. Tony agreed to pay the equivalent of the man's wages for as long as they were together. The guide's name was Ricaurte.

Two days later they set off, each carrying a backpack weighing some thirty pounds, filled not only with the minimal amount of clothing required, but also food and three bottles of aguardiente each to use as barter. They walked for four hours before stopping by a river for a lunch of fried yuca, rice and tinned frankfurters. Already Tony's feet ached and his legs were trembling, but these minor setbacks were compensated by some of the most beautiful scenery he had ever seen.

Apart from isolated adobe houses with patches of maize, it seemed completely deserted. As they climbed higher, the maize gave way to potato fields, but, although occasionally they spotted another person walking towards them in the distance, they never crossed paths. Tony assumed the other person had left the path and hidden in the bushes until they were past.

In the early afternoon they stopped at a small school run by nuns, who gave them lemonade, soup and coffee, and by evening they reached a pretty Indian village called Timbuchuque: half a dozen adobe houses made of mud and bamboo perched on a hilltop, all with their doors closed. Ricaurte approached one and started speaking softly through it, then listening, then repeating himself, until eventually the door opened a crack and a face peered out. Ricaurte kept reassuring the man that they came in peace, there was nothing to fear, that Tony was not from the government, in fact was not even Colombian, until eventually the man stepped out, closing the door behind him.

Prompted by Ricaurte, Tony produced a bottle of aguardiente and some tinned ham, and offered it to the man, who accepted it gratefully and smiled. Then the man called out, and the door of his house reopened. Out stepped a woman and three small children, all barefoot.

Tony and Ricaurte were invited inside the small house, where a clay pot of locally made chicha, a maize-based alcohol mixed with panela, hard brown sugar, was produced. The floor was hard mud, uncovered; cobs of maize hung from the rafters, and the smoke from the small fire simply seeped through the thatched roof to escape. They explained that they didn't make chimneys because it was too cold in winter, so they sat with eyes smarting from the smoke before eating a simple dinner of maize fritters, beans and rice and, like birds, went to sleep on the dirt floor as soon as the sun set and plunged them into darkness.

Tony and Ricaurte walked through the mountains for twelve days, up and down zigzag paths, climbing peaks and descending into deep, narrow valleys, where often they washed under waterfalls and drank from crystal clear streams. Midway through, Tony fell ill, probably from contaminated chicha the night before. Ricaurte took his backpack without complaint as Tony vomited repeatedly or kept diving into the undergrowth to relieve his diarrhoea, but they kept going for a full eight hours, and fortunately by the next day the crisis had passed.

Their last stop in the village of Lamé was the best of all. There was a circle of around twenty houses around a white colonial church, with the village laid out on a bright green lawn on a ledge halfway up a mountain. Once they were past the now customary persuasions to get people to open their doors, they were invited into the home of the headman, a man called Feliciano. It was larger than other houses they had stayed in, with a small kitchen area at the back, and two bedrooms on either side of the main communal room. Although they were poor, the hospitality they offered was overwhelming, sharing a meal of rice, eggs and beans before Feliciano insisted Tony and Ricaurte take their beds, while he and his family slept on the floor. Tony didn't want to accept, but Ricaurte said a refusal would be insulting.

Tony was the first foreigner the family had ever seen, and they were fascinated by his stories of the world outside, even though they said they wouldn't want to change their ways, or allow outsiders to live amongst them. Their independence outranked all other considerations, and they were determined to do things their own way. They were not against progress, they said; they would happily accept schools or hospitals in their community, but they wanted the teachers, doctors and nurses to be Páez.

Grey skies and heavy rain meant that they stayed in Lamé the next day. It became cold; there was no sign of the sun. The clouds were impenetrable, shrouding the tops of even the nearest mountains, and, as the rain began to seep through the thatched roof and puddle on the floor, they sat hunched in their ruanas, the Colombian version of a poncho, drinking chicha and talking. Tony felt uncomfortable about spending a second night with Feliciano, worried that their presence would overtax their host's limited resources, even though they gave him the last of their tinned food, and the only surviving bottle of aguardiente.

As if by magic, the sky cleared suddenly in mid-afternoon, revealing the glistening white top of the Nevado de Huila volcano. Shortly afterwards a priest rode into the village to hold mass the next day, when it would be Ash Wednesday, and two rockets were fired into the air to inform people in the surrounding area of his arrival. In the interests of a quiet life, the Páez paid lip service to Catholicism, even if, as the priest probably knew, they set more store by their local shaman.

Their last night was clear and starlit, and the next morning Ricaurte and Tony said their farewells to Feliciano and Lamé after a breakfast of scrambled eggs and began the long trek back to 'civilisation'. They passed a couple more small villages but didn't stop, and they ate nothing because they had no more food; they just drank water from the streams and walked for ten hours before reaching the small town of Belacázar. Tony felt a great sadness descend upon him as they dodged cars in the town's streets; already he missed the heavenly quiet of Tierradentro.

After grabbing a couple of empanadas, they plodded on for another six miles to the Páez River bridge and caught a lift in the back of a truck for the next three miles to El Crucao, from where they could walk the last two miles to San Andrés de Pisimbalá. Tony found that, after learning the slow high-stepping walk of the jungle, he had now developed 'mountain legs' with the curious long, loping stride of the locals, which enabled him to walk for hours without a break.

They were spotted long before they arrived. Children ran down the road shouting their names and, when they reached the village, they were astonished to find a raucous fiesta in their honour in full swing inside the small shop which doubled as a bar.

After nearly fifteen hours on the road Tony's feet were sore, his flea bites were itching and his clothes, with days of dried sweat, felt as stiff as cardboard, but, as the beer and aguardiente flowed, he felt his tiredness lift and he quickly joined in the singing and dancing. Another big surprise was the discovery of several other travellers present, who regarded him with some awe. One, a pretty French-Canadian girl called Adele, came up to him and kissed him on both cheeks.

'Welcome back,' she said. 'You've made quite a name for yourself!'

She was petite, with ice-blue eyes and yellow-blond hair above a triangular face, and wore beautiful Indian embroidered clothes.

They spent the next three days together, wandering amongst the tombs, discovering new ones every day, and in the evenings held each other tight. 'I haven't been held like that in a long time,' Adele said on the first morning. She was travelling to try to get over the death of her fiancé in a car accident in Canada, and was on her way to La Paz to meet friends.

'I've just come from La Paz,' Tony told her. 'It's a bit rough, to be honest. Why not change your plans? We can travel together.'

She looked into his eyes. 'Part of me would like that very much. But it's too soon, I'm not ready for another relationship yet, but maybe we can stay in touch? I'll write to you.'

And so, after three days, they went their separate ways: Adele to Bolivia, while Tony retraced his tracks to Bogotá. Like ships in the night, Tony thought, but maybe it was better that way.

He took a cab from El Dorado airport back to Bill's house, where the maid opened the door for him. He found Bill in the lounge watching television.

'I'm back!' Tony announced. 'And now I can speak Spanish: pure Castellano, in fact!'

Bill rose from the sofa and howled with laughter. 'You sound like a fucking campesino!' he said. 'But never mind, we can soon iron that out. What's next?'

'Next is we need to have a talk. First, I'll go to the poste restante tomorrow to see if anything has changed in Brazil. If not, then I need to think about your proposal, maybe?'

'Take your time; we have plenty of it. Tonight, let's just enjoy ourselves.'

'With some postre?'

CHAPTER NINETEEN

Newspapers

There was a letter from Roberto, but again it was not good news. He'd been 'advised' by the police to leave Rondônia, so he had returned to his home state of Rio Grande do Sul. Water Flower Garden and Rio Novo had both been put up for sale and were in the process of being purchased by a Japanese-led consortium. The police were also still looking for Tony, so there was no point in him returning to the country for now. Of Conceição, there was no word.

'You know people in the States?' Bill asked Tony when he had returned, as they sat in his study.

'Sure, some. An old girlfriend in New York, a guy in Minneapolis, and one in North Carolina, but he's a bit strange. Actually, everyone in North Carolina seemed a bit strange to me. Oh, and a guy I went to college with who lives in Florida.'

'Hmm, we'll stay away from Florida for now.' Bill passed him a rolled newspaper with a strip of paper around the middle for an address. 'Tell me, what do you see here? Look at it carefully.'

Tony took the newspaper; it was a copy of *El Tiempo*, the biggest newspaper in the country. He studied it, turned it around, then looked at one end and the other, squeezing the package so he could see inside, but there was nothing. 'Looks like a newspaper ready for posting to me,' he said. 'But I'm sure you're going to tell me it's something else.'

'Right, a newspaper for the post is what it's supposed to look like,' Bill replied, taking the newspaper back from him. 'And in fact, that's what it is. But now, watch.' With a knife, he carefully slit the postal wrapping open, and just as carefully unwrapped the newspaper, which had been folded in such a way that nothing was visible from the outside from either end, no matter how much you squeezed it. In the centre was a slim plastic package of white powder.

'Fifty grams,' Bill announced. 'When it's cut it'll be seventy or seventy-five. Cost fifty dollars here; if we sell at fifty dollars a gram that will be nearly $4,000. By the time it hits the street in the US it's more like seventy or eighty dollars a gram, so everyone wins, and there's hardly any risk.'

'Show me how you do it, from the beginning,' Tony said.

'Okay, first you need one of these,' Bill explained, producing a slim electric machine for sealing the plastic bag. 'You've got to make sure you get all the air out, and of course make sure the seal is good. The smaller the package, the better.' He then showed Tony the complex way to fold the inner pages of the newspaper where the package would be hidden, so that nothing was visible from either end. 'Here, you try.'

Tony tried to copy Bill's movements, but the first two attempts were unsuccessful; from either end of the package the plastic package was visible. Bill showed him again, how he was folding the inner pages wrong, and finally he managed to master the technique.

'So where do we send them?' Tony asked.

'We can start with your friends in the States. But don't put their names on the address, and you must insist they don't open the newspapers, or magazines, whatever we're sending. Just leave them unopened near the front door or something.'

'Why is that?'

'Because it gives them total deniability. If for any reason the cops get suspicious and come knocking, they can just say they've no idea who the newspaper is for, that it's probably a wrong address, and they were meaning to throw it away.'

'What about England?'

'We can do that too. A bit further to travel, but I do know someone who can move the stuff there.'

They eventually came up with a shortlist of six addresses they could use across the United States, and a further five in England.

The occupants of all were told that Tony was sending back a series of newspaper and magazine articles to help him with research on a book he was writing. They were given strict instructions not to open the packages. Although a few eyebrows were raised when he said the mail would not be in his name, he explained that the subject matter was sensitive and he needed to keep his name disguised, and eventually they all accepted the explanation.

Over the next three months they sent out at least ten packages a week, each containing fifty or sometimes seventy-five grams of pure cocaine, which amounted to some six kilograms of the drug, netting them a profit of around $200,000 after expenses. It was the early 1980s, the global cocaine trade was still in its relatively early days, and attempts by law enforcement to get on top of it were largely focussed on the big players, like Escobar and Lehder. No one was checking mail much, and there were no sniffer dogs in the sorting offices: it was almost comically easy, as long as they kept a low profile. Until they got careless and made some silly mistakes.

Tony's main role in the operation was to travel to the United States and deliver the merchandise to the buyers, and once Bill joined him for a trip to London to introduce him to a buyer who lived in Maida Vale and would take all they could deliver. They visited museums and ate in fine restaurants, and Tony also dropped into a national newspaper and the BBC's World Service radio in the Aldwych, where he picked up a couple of strings and letters of accreditation, which would help him obtain a temporary resident's permit back in Bogotá. They also rented a small flat under a false name in Peckham, which would be a perfect address for deliveries.

The problem was that by the time they were six months into their enterprise, Tony had developed quite a fondness for his own product, and had started shovelling up to a gram a day up his nose. It meant he started carrying a small phial of the stuff with him wherever he went, which was idiotic in the extreme, and, sure enough, as he sat in a parked car outside a nightclub in Cincinnati enjoying a snort, the car door was suddenly yanked open and he was hauled out by a huge uniformed cop. He hadn't even been watching out; he hadn't even locked the car door!

In a split-second reaction, Tony somehow had the presence of mind to fling the glass phial into the road, and then the satisfaction of seeing it crushed under the wheels of a passing car, destroying the evidence, but the cop still slammed a pair of handcuffs on him and threw him into the back of a squad car.

Tony was stunned. He was as high as a kite and couldn't grasp what was happening to him, as if he were in some kind of nightmare but would soon wake up and everything would be fine again. Except it wasn't.

At the police station he was kept in a cell for several hours. The cops were furious that they had no evidence, and called him a 'fucking Limey' and other choice names as they threw accusations at him, while he remained silent. Eventually they decided to take him downtown to the 'Workhouse', a primitive prison that had been condemned a decade before and had housed prisoners during the American Civil War more than a hundred years earlier, while they thought about their next move.

On the plus side, it wasn't a hardcore state penitentiary, but more of a holding centre while prisoners waited for a bail hearing or trial for minor misdemeanours. From the outside it didn't look too bad: a large white building and one of the oldest around, which by itself lent it a certain charm. But inside it was something of a horror show from another age; rats and cockroaches ran freely across the floors, where there were also puddles from the leaking roof.

There were several blocks, with maybe six ranges of forty cells each, and in every cell a bucket for ablutions, and a straw mattress. At least it was just one prisoner to a cell, which Tony was happy about given the stories told about US prisons.

The guards were mostly young and were a mixture of the corrupt, the bullying and the sympathetic. The other inmates were a mixed bag of old timers and young bloods, some accused of assault, others of theft or sex or drug offences, or just traffic violations. They included 'Red', with his thin orange beard, and 'Hatchet', and 'No

Legs', an amputee veteran of Vietnam, and 'Art', a young black man with wiry hair tied in knots and an ugly scar running the length of one cheek.

Tony felt utter despair; he couldn't believe that only a few months earlier he'd been hiking in the mountains of Tierradentro, free as a bird, and now his wings had been suddenly clipped and he'd been plunged into the unknown. He understood now that no one who hadn't experienced prison, or the loss of their freedom, could truly understand the emotions it triggered, the terrible emptiness of each day, the desperation and the loneliness.

The television was switched on at 7 pm, and the inmates sat on their beds watching through the criss-cross wires of their cells, waiting for sleep and oblivion, but not wanting to sleep too early for fear of waking in the dark hours, alone and cold, with just a distant ghostly neon light streaming in through the bars. Breakfast was cold potatoes, lunch spam sandwiches and beans, and every day they hoped for something better, and every day they were disappointed.

Tony was left to cool his heels for three days, before the police finally accepted that they had no grounds to hold him longer, and reluctantly allowed him to go free, with the warning that he should fuck off out of the country and that they would be watching him until he did. Tony took their advice, and resolved to renounce any further illegal activity, or at least anything to do with the cocaine trade. He felt that it had been a warning from above, and that this time his guardian angel had looked out for him, but he wasn't going to push his luck.

CHAPTER TWENTY

Los Llanos

Tony decided, however, to return to Colombia. He liked the country not just for the spectacular scenery, the food and the friends he had made, but also for its sense of anarchy which, despite some of the inherent dangers it implied, was also a kind of freedom compared to the stifling overregulation of life in Europe or the United States. It was also closer to Brazil, which he still hoped to revisit when possible.

First, though, he returned to London to put his affairs in order. He found a country still basking in the afterglow of victory in the Falklands War and a booming economy. Christmas parties were in full swing, and on the last night of the year, after hooking up with some old friends, Tony went with them to Trafalgar Square, armed with bottles of champagne, to dance with strangers, sing 'Auld Lang Syne', and generally get shitfaced as they welcomed in 1983.

'1984 next year, lads!' Tony shouted as the last of Big Ben's bongs faded away. 'Wonder if George Orwell was right?' Little did he realise then how prescient a book *Nineteen Eighty-Four* would prove to be, but that it would just take a bit longer for some of the predictions to come to fruition.

Before leaving the country, Tony visited the newspaper and the BBC World Service to renew his stringer agreements, and then took a tour of a small fish farm in Surrey, where he commissioned a business plan to be drawn up for a similar venture in Colombia. He was convinced that a regular supply of fresh trout to Bogotá's better restaurants could be a real winner.

Bogotá was not a warm city; it was too high for that and was often shrouded in cloud, but after January in London it was a relief to get back. Tony's first port of call was a two-week holiday on the island of San Andrés in the Caribbean, a paradise back then before overdevelopment took over, and closer to Nicaragua and Panama than Colombia, but apparently the French had kindly given it to Colombia hundreds of years ago for some reason. Maybe because Panama was part of Colombia back then.

Next, he rented a small apartment on Calle 82, just above Carrera 45. He focused on his new alias as a freelance reporter with his work permit and temporary residency papers in place, and scouted around for some land to buy where he could establish his fish farm. Needless to say, both Bill and Isobel thought he was quite mad.

'It'll just swallow your money. You don't understand. Even if the fish survive, people will steal them,' Isobel told him.

Tony shrugged. 'Maybe, maybe not. If it works, it could be a real money spinner. And anyway, I just fancy it; it gives me something to do and will keep me out of mischief. It'll be a first in Colombia.'

'Fucking crazy man,' was Bill's contribution. 'So where are thinking of putting this English folly of yours?'

'It's got to be somewhere with a river or stream running through the land. Not too high up, because I don't want to be freezing my arse off all the time. And not too far from Bogotá, obviously, given that this place will be my main market.'

In the end, Tony settled on a small farm near the town of Acacías, less than an hour beyond the much larger city of Villavicencio, which itself lay at the bottom of the Andes Eastern Cordillera some seventy miles away from Bogotá. Villavicencio also marked the beginnings of Los Llanos, the eastern plains, and boasted an airport as well as a number of industries.

In all, the farm covered just over forty acres and had a small but fast and tree-lined stream running the length of the land. However, although it wasn't so far from the capital city, the narrow, winding mountain road meant it was a good four-hour drive away.

The farm cost him just $15,000, and he spent the same again on two circular tanks ten metres in diameter, nets, lids for the tanks, pumps, aerators, a filtration system, automatic feeders, hatchery troughs and baskets, pipe works and monitoring devices, such as a water testing kit and thermometers, all imported from the United States. With the help of some local labour, he built a large shed where he could keep the tanks, and pumped water from the stream to fill them up. Finally, again from the United States, he ordered 200 Nile tilapia hatchlings, which he had decided were better suited than trout to the conditions of Los Llanos. Trout, it seemed, needed much cooler water and were more susceptible to diseases, while tilapia, still a very tasty fish, preferred a water temperature of around 29°C, were more resistant to illness and were ready for the table within about six months, so promised better profits.

The farmhouse was basic but adequate, with two bedrooms, a kitchen, a lounge area and a veranda where Tony could sit in the evenings with a cold beer and listen to the chorus of frogs. For electricity he had two generators, one for the house and the second for the shed housing the fish tanks.

The icing on the cake, though, was the local girl he hired to work as his housemaid, because it wasn't long before she was substantially more than that. Mercedes had arrived at the farm one day, barefoot, and asked if he needed a maid. She was a dream find: a black-haired classic, small and slim, who could not only cook but also enjoyed gardening, creating a small herb garden, and she took a keen interest in the fish farming.

When Tony asked where her family were and where she was from, she just shrugged and told him it was 'the war'. He wasn't sure what war she was referring to, but either way he was starting to really enjoy life once more and appreciated having another chance to put down roots, and he didn't probe.

He had a car, a second-hand Daihatsu jeep, for when he needed to go to Bogotá, but locally he and Mercedes tended to ride their two horses when they wanted to visit Acacías for general stores, such as rice and flour, coffee or sugar. He absolutely loved riding into town with Mercedes at his side and tying up the horses like in an old Western movie outside the general store, then taking a coffee or beer on the sidewalk before collecting his order, loading up the horses and returning along the track to his farm.

Bill and Isobel came to visit and were duly impressed. 'I never thought you'd do it,' Bill said, watching the fish tanks' occupants rise to the water's surface as Tony threw some feed in. He also brought some good news: he'd managed to persuade four restaurants in Bogotá to give the fish a try, which, added to the two Tony himself had found in Villavicencio, was a good start.

'But how long will you do this for?' Isobel wanted to know. 'Aren't you bored down here, with no one except campesinos to talk to?'

Tony laughed. 'Well, as least I talk like them, so they understand me! But seriously, the thing is that I'm happy, I feel free, and I don't mind not having a lot of company. And anyway, if I can make a success of the business and one day find I've had enough, I'll have an asset to sell. It doesn't have to be forever.'

Within a year the business was thriving, and after two years he'd added two more fish tanks, doubling his output, and had hired two labourers to help with the workload. He was beginning to wonder if he'd spend the rest of his days there, if he'd actually found his own personal paradise again, when disaster struck.

CHAPTER TWENTY-ONE

M-19

They came shortly before dawn, walking silently through a dense mist that covered the field in front of the house: half a dozen men and women in camouflage, heavily armed. One banged on the door while the others stood in a semicircle on the grass. 'Open up!'

'What the fuck?' Tony stumbled into his dungarees and grabbed his shotgun. 'Who's there?'

'Movimiento 19 de Abril, in the name of the people! Open up, no one gets hurt!'

Gingerly Tony opened the door a crack, Mercedes at his shoulder. 'Puta!' she hissed. 'This is not good.'

'What do you want?' Tony asked.

'Put the gun down. You have to come with us. As I said, no one gets hurt.' He was a young man, bespectacled and with dark stubble on his face, a green bandana around his head.

'What do you want with us?'

'Please, no questions, just come with us.'

Tony realised he had no choice. He slowly lowered the shotgun and raised his hands in the air.

He and Mercedes were marched to the road, where two vans waited with engines running, the drivers smoking furiously, and they were pushed into the back of one of the vehicles. A little over an hour later they stopped outside an apartment building in Villavicencio and the pair were bundled upstairs to the top floor, which had two apartments, both M-19 safe houses. They were separated, with Tony being led into one apartment, and Mercedes the other.

'You've got the wrong guy,' Tony told them when he was ordered to sit at a table. 'What do you want with me?'

'What's a gringo doing here?' the bespectacled man asked him. 'Some say you are a spy for the CIA.'

'Who are you?'

'You can call me Aureliano.'

'Aureliano? Like the character in *One Hundred Years of Solitude*?'

The man chuckled. 'Very good! So, you like to read Gabriel García Márquez?'

'Sometimes. He's pretty good. Maybe not all his books, but that one, yes.'

'He is a good man; he's on our side, you know. But we digress. You haven't answered my question; what are you doing here?'

Tony sighed and stretched out his legs, ran a hand through his long hair. 'First of all, I'm not a gringo as you say. I'm English. I'm here because I like the place, I've built a fish farm, as you probably know. It's hard work, but it's a good business.'

'Some people say you are a spy.' Aureliano offered him a cigarette and lit it for him. 'Would you like a coffee?'

Tony was confused. It was all very civilised, but threatening at the same time. He had no idea which way it was going to go. 'What people? Of course I'm not a fucking spy, what would I be spying on down here? The fish?'

'You move around. We know you go to Bogotá often, and here to Villavicencio. Who do you meet?'

'I go to Bogotá to sell fish, for God's sake! And I have some friends there. Is that a crime?'

'We can't be too careful; there are enemies everywhere. Maybe you are keeping track of people's movements, reporting them.'

'Everyone has enemies. You're just being paranoid, I came here to get away from everything and live a quiet life, that's all. You have nothing to fear from me.'

Aureliano stubbed out his cigarette and left the room. Tony heard the door to the next apartment being opened and closed again. He wondered what was happening to Mercedes, but he needn't have worried.

It turned out that the guerrillas holding them were mostly ex-students disgusted by the corruption in the country. Their ideology was one of nationalism and their aim to open up electoral democracy in the country, which made them a far cry from other rebel groups in the country such as FARC and the ELN, who had ideologies closer to communism and whose members were mainly drawn from the campesinos in the countryside. M-19 were an urban-oriented group, again unlike FARC and the ELN, who tended to stick to the jungles.

It was three days before Aureliano, apparently the leader of the group, returned. During that time Tony was well treated, given a mattress to sleep on and regular meals, but he was pissed off. It felt too much like prison again; well, it *was* a prison, given that he'd been kidnapped and held against his will. He also knew full well that M-19 had kidnapped hundreds of people for ransom, although mostly drug traffickers, businessmen and politicians. It was one of their main sources of finance. They were also known to execute suspected CIA spies.

Aureliano looked tired, but he gave Tony a reassuring smile. 'Okay, we accept that you're not working for the CIA. But we do know you have been working for the media, even the BBC, and they are not our friends. We don't think you should stay here. Actually, if you do, we think your life will be in danger, although not from us.'

'From who, then?'

'Ah, that is a complicated question. There are so many groups here: guerrillas, drug traffickers, paramilitaries like MAS – Muerte a Secuestradores, Death to Kidnappers. A gringo in the middle of it all can always be a target.'

'I told you before, I'm not a gringo.'

'Okay, okay,' Aureliano laughed, 'but I don't think most of the people I'm talking about will, how do you say, split hairs about that.'

Tony stared at him, thinking. 'What about my woman, Mercedes; what have you done with her?'

'Oh, she is fine. In fact, she wants to join us. Did you know her parents were victims of MAS?'

'I didn't know that; she never told me. But I'd like to speak to her.'

'You will, my friend, you will.'

'I'm not your friend. And what about my farm?'

'Ah, I'm afraid it now belongs to the revolution. We have sequestered it. I am sorry.'

'That's theft! I built that business up from nothing!' Tony had raised his voice.

'And it will be put to good use, I assure you. Think of it as a gift to the people. We will take you back there to collect your personal things, and we will then take you to Bogotá. Just be glad that it was us, and not one of the other groups, that took you. We try to be civilised, but we are at war.'

'That's what Mercedes said,' Tony muttered, his shoulders slumped. He could see no way out of this.

'And she is right. Again, I am sorry.'

As they returned to the farm in the vans early the following day, Mercedes held Tony's hand. 'I am sorry, Tony,' she said. 'I will look after the farm for you, I don't want to see you go, but it is for the best; these are dangerous times. I also don't want to leave Colombia.'

Tony nodded. 'Everyone keeps saying they're fucking sorry, but I'm the one getting robbed!'

They said their farewells after Tony had collected his belongings, and, most importantly, his passport. Aureliano and three of the others, two women and a man, plus Mercedes, stayed at the farm, and Tony watched them fade into the distance as he was driven back to the capital by two other men. Many years later, 'Aureliano' was elected as president of Colombia, and Tony learned his real name.

CHAPTER TWENTY-TWO

Back to Brazil and Beyond

Returned safely to Bogotá, but with his ego bruised, Tony gave notice on his small flat and went to tell Bill and Isobel what had happened, and that he was planning on leaving the country.

'Poor you,' Isobel said, placing a tray with coffee and cups on the table. 'You seem to be getting hounded out of one place and another. It's not fair.'

'Fair doesn't come into it,' Tony replied. 'It just is what it is. I think I'll go back to Brazil first, then I'll see. There just doesn't seem to be much point in staying on here for the time being; I mean, what would I do? At least I didn't lose on the farm in Acacías; it was making a good profit and had paid me back my investment, and some.'

'And those M-19 guys were probably right,' Bill put in. 'Better them than some of the other bad guys. It was kind of bound to happen sooner or later. You know the country is going through a bad time, not a good place to be a gringo right now.'

'I'm not a fucking gringo!'

Bill laughed. 'But you're easy to wind up. Come on, tonight we party, tomorrow we'll see.'

And party they did, for two days solid, after which Bill dropped a drained Tony off at El Dorado airport. 'You take care, my friend. You know you are always welcome back, but I don't think we will ever see each other again.'

'Don't be daft, of course we'll see each other again.'

But Bill was right. When Tony boarded his Avianca flight to Rio de Janeiro, where he connected for another to Porto Alegre, the capital of Rio Grande do Sul, it would be the last he would see of

Bogotá.

He spent Christmas and New Year of 1986 with Roberto, during which time they enjoyed an emotional reunion, reminiscing about their time in Rondônia together, and wondering what had happened to Conceição. Porto Alegre was a big city, around a million people, and the southernmost state capital in Brazil, lying at the confluence of five rivers which together formed a giant freshwater lagoon, the Lagoa dos Patos. Roberto was studying to be a lawyer.

'You never thought about going back to Amazonia, then?' Tony asked him as they sat on the pavement outside a café, drinking cold Brahma Chopp beers.

'I did, for a while.' Roberto hunched forwards and stared at the ground, then looked up. 'But then I realised it was over. Water Flower Garden was a dream, yes, a kind of paradise like we always said, but after that business with de Brito it felt tainted, like it would never be the same again, and I just didn't have the energy at the time to start over again. I guess we change as we get older, ambitions change.'

'It's a shame; I was happy there for a while. I actually thought I'd found my purpose in life, you know?'

'Yes, but you should also know that Rondônia is becoming one of the most deforested areas of the Amazon jungle. Thousands and thousands of square miles of forest are being destroyed every year. Mostly it's for cattle farming, but they are also mining, for tin ore, gold, manganese, iron, you name it. If they keep this up, at some point the forest will collapse in on itself and transition into scrubby savannah.'

'Which means?'

'Which means the Amazon would no longer be able to store carbon, you know, to counter climate change. Remember, the Amazon is half of all the rainforests in the world.'

'So instead of a jungle, you could end up with something more like a desert?'

'It's true. The topsoil in the jungle is very thin; if it gets washed away because there are no trees to protect it, then you are left with very poor soil. It will happen, but I won't be there to see it. It was good while it lasted, but that adventure is over for me now.'

'And you're going to be a lawyer? Won't that bore you shitless?'

Roberto grimaced and took a long slug of his beer. 'Maybe. This is a nice city, the weather is good, and the sea is not far. Perhaps I'll find a wife and settle down to a boring little life, who knows?'

'What happened to Raimunda?'

'Ah, she went back to Porto Velho. The city was not for her. And what about you?'

Tony shrugged. 'Not sure, to be honest. Probably time I gave South America a break. I was thinking of taking a look at South Africa, and if I don't like that, then maybe Australia. I'm a bit lost, to be honest. Again.'

A week later he found himself in Cape Town, and thinking he'd made a big mistake. It was a beautiful city in parts, but elsewhere it was a no-go zone. The country was under a state of emergency, and every day seemed to bring more killings; grenades were thrown, limpet mines exploded, and hotels were attacked as the apartheid era neared its end, and Nelson Mandela neared the end of his twenty-seven years in prison. Tony decided it was no place to be looking for work or settling down for a while; it wasn't his fight. But he was advised by an employment agency to maybe approach an oil company that was hiring people to work in Nigeria, where the oil business was booming.

'Nigeria? Isn't that a bit like out of the frying pan and into the fire?'

'It's the big beast of Africa, lots of potential there, and the oil business is huge,' the employment agency man told Tony. 'Here, I'll give you the address of the company that's hiring if you like, and send them a message to expect you.'

'I don't really know West Africa at all.'

'It's very different from here, and you'll need a visa, but if you get the job that would all be sorted. And the pay is good.'

So it was that, a couple of days later, Tony found himself being interviewed for a job about which he knew next to nothing.

'You've worked in the oil business before, have you?' asked the interviewer, a burly man with a huge ginger beard and a strong Boer accent.

'Sure, yes, I did a couple of years up on the North Sea oilfields,' Tony lied.

'Doing what?'

'Well, mostly warehouse stuff in fact: checking stock, organising deliveries, that sort of thing. I wasn't actually out on the rigs much.'

The big man studied Tony's letter of application and grunted. 'Well, we've got an opening for a depot manager in Port Harcourt, if that's of any interest? We could hire locally, but corruption is a big problem in Nigeria, so we'd prefer a Westerner in charge of the depot. Otherwise, half the stock would probably disappear.'

'I'm interested.'

'Got any references?'

'I can get them, but it'd probably take a while. Why don't I get them sent to Nigeria?'

'Hmmm. It's a bit irregular, but you seem an okay kind of guy, so consider yourself hired.' And he rose and held out a meaty fist for Tony to shake, glad to have found someone willing to take on the challenges of Port Harcourt.

Tony arrived ten days later once his visa was in place. He flew from Johannesburg with South African Airways to Murtala Muhammed International Airport in Lagos, named after some assassinated military dictator about a decade earlier, and caught a connecting flight to Port Harcourt, where he was met by a company rep.

Port Harcourt was a huge sprawling city of more than three million people lying on the Bonny River, and the sweltering heat made Tony feel like he had walked into a gigantic sauna, the air sucked from his lungs. It was humid as hell, in stark contrast to his recent stay in Colombia, but not so distinct from the suffocating heat of the Amazon, except that here the air wasn't fresh; the sense was of vegetation rotting instead of growing exuberantly. It was known as the Garden City, and there were plenty of flowers and trees, but plenty of rubbish too. Discarded plastic bags were ubiquitous, and some of the streets they drove through were foetid, but then they drove past a Cadbury's factory and the air filled with the smell of sweet chocolate. Fortunately, they had air conditioning.

The company rep was a small, wiry Italian called Marcello, a pipeline engineer, who seemed to exude pent-up aggression and barely suppressed violence. His last job had been a three-year stint in Norway where his family had joined him, but this time he'd left his wife and two daughters behind in Italy as he didn't think Port Harcourt was a suitable place for a family. His dream was to get a cushy job in one of the Gulf states: the UAE or Qatar or Bahrain or even Oman, maybe. Meanwhile he had to put up with Nigeria, fidgeting furiously as he sat with Tony in the back of the big white Toyota Land Cruiser, while a local called Tunde took the wheel.

The traffic was appalling and there were people everywhere, a mass of humanity going about their daily struggle for survival, but they seemed cheerful enough. Several waved at Tony and called out, 'Hey, Whitey, what you doing here?' and he waved back and wondered if he'd get away with shouting 'hey, Blackie' at Africans in the streets of London. It was mostly low-rise, timber-framed houses with corrugated iron roofs, apart from the office blocks and industrial areas. Above all, he found he was enjoying that sense of anarchy which had previously so attracted him to Colombia, and he thought he might actually be able to adapt to life in Port Harcourt.

'Never drive yourself here,' Marcello told him. 'If you have an accident, even a little bump, they will blame you for everything, fake injuries, and try and take you to the cleaners.'

'How will I get around, then?'

'We have a pool of cars and drivers, and there's a few of us that live in the same compound where I'm taking you, so getting to work is not a problem.'

'What about the evenings? If I want to go out?'

'Oh, you can always book a driver, that's what they are paid for, but it's worth giving them some naira as a tip every now and again.

Keeps them sweet. Anyway, I wouldn't recommend wandering around the streets at night on your own.'

They drew up at a new gated apartment block at the far end of Peter Odili Road, one of the main thoroughfares, near the crossing over a creek to the Trans Amadi residential area. Marcello showed Tony into a compact one-bedroom apartment on the fourth floor, which had a small balcony overlooking a swimming pool at the back. There was a kitchen and bathroom, plus a lounge equipped with a television.

'It's not much, but it's quite a good area,' Marcello said. 'We have half a dozen apartments in the block. And there's a canteen at the port if you don't fancy cooking all the time. Anyway, I'll let you rest and see you at work tomorrow.'

'I think it'd be best if I did some shopping first,' Tony said. 'At least get some beers in the fridge.'

'Take Tunde, then; he'll know where to go and bring you back. I've got the rest of the day off, but I'm in number 602, two floors up, if you need anything.'

The next day Tony was driven with Marcello to the port and shown to a small office on the mezzanine of the company's warehouse. 'So, this is your kingdom,' Marcello announced. 'Most of the other expats, myself included, spend our days out in the field. I've told the warehouse staff to gather round in half an hour when we'll introduce you. There's about thirty of them.'

At least the office was air-conditioned, while the port itself was impressive, a steaming hive of activity with both boat building and fishing industries and a deep-water harbour to handle the export of palm oil, timber, tin and, of course, petroleum. Pipelines carried the oil from the fields in the eastern Niger River delta straight to the port, and also to the port of Bonny about twenty-five miles away. With huge oil reserves, Nigeria had become one of the top producers worldwide, with the black gold accounting for more than ninety percent of the country's exports and a big chunk of its gross domestic product.

As the depot manager, Tony's job was fairly straightforward. All he really had to do was manage the staff, monitor the receipt or issuing of products, ensure the safe storage and distribution of things like pipelines, tanks and fuel sampling gadgets, check valves, pumps and other equipment associated with the bulk handling of petroleum liquids, and above all keep his nose clean and make sure there was no fiddling of the books, theft or corruption.

He settled in easily. The staff were generally indolent, but they gave a good impression of seeming to work, even when they weren't doing much. Even the way they walked mystified Tony; it was so slow it seemed more of an effort than walking at a normal pace. If they'd walked any slower, they'd have been going backwards. Almost all were shaven-headed, and they greeted him as 'boss' with a small bow of the head, which he found disconcerting at first. It helped, though, that they all spoke English, even if amongst themselves they more generally reverted to Pidgin. The humid heat meant it wasn't long before Tony also had his long locks shorn off, although he stopped short of the full razor treatment, preferring an old-style short back and sides instead.

After work, once the warehouse had been secured and Tony had been driven back to his apartment block, he often ignored Marcello's cautious advice and walked out in the area around Peter Odili Road, which he'd discovered offered numerous restaurants, both local and international, as well as bars and local shops. He developed a taste for a local favourite, bole, a delicacy made from roast yam, plantain and meat stew. He avoided quiet side roads, but otherwise didn't feel unsafe. Apart from the Muslim north of the country, Nigerians in general didn't have a reputation for murdering Westerners: robbing them, yes, but unlike in South Africa they rarely resorted to violence.

In April the rainy season set in. Local creeks flooded, the roads were often under several inches of water, walking under the heavy downfalls became virtually impossible, the traffic was even worse, and life in general became much more difficult. It would last six months.

More worrying than the weather, however, were reports coming from the north of the country of serious riots and inter-religious violence. According to media reports, a Muslim woman had slapped a Christian pastor she accused of misinterpreting the Koran in the majority Christian southern part of Kaduna state, and within days eight Koranic teachers were dead, seven with their throats cut and one shot with an arrow.

It was made worse by the fact that the Christians and Muslims were often from different ethnic groups. In the days that followed, in the mostly Muslim areas around the city of Kaduna itself, students went on the rampage, burning dozens of churches and killing fifteen or twenty random people. Christian businesses were also burnt to the ground, and even hotels that served beer.

The Biafran civil war of the late 1960s, during which some two million generally Catholic Igbos in the Niger Delta region starved to death, mostly at the hands of the Muslim Hausa-dominated military, was still fresh in many people's minds, and for a time people feared the worst. No one wanted a return to a full-scale civil war, and fortunately this time the government responded robustly and the violence was stamped out, despite an ongoing simmering resentment between the two sides.

But as the trouble in the north was damped down, the Niger Delta itself began to have its own problem, and this time the oil industry was the target. Theft of oil by petty criminals had always been a problem, people puncturing the pipes carrying the oil to siphon some off for the black market, but it was a minor irritant rather than a major disruption, despite the environmental havoc caused by the spillages. But as the 1980s ended the oil companies faced a much more serious threat from a variety of protest groups such as the Movement for the Survival of the Ogoni People, or MOSOP, and the more violent Movement for the Emancipation of the Niger Delta, or MEND.

These groups wanted to expose the oppression of the region's people and the devastation of the environment. The fishing industry had been decimated, but precious little of the money derived from the oil business trickled down to the street, despite a revenue sharing plan under which the federal government was supposed to distribute around half of the country's total oil revenues through the state governors. Most of that money seemed to stay with the state governors and their entourage. Nigeria's own anti-corruption body estimated that up to three quarters of the country's oil revenues were either stolen or wasted. Protest groups wanted reparations to be paid, and, through a mixture of non-violent protest and, later, sabotage, guerrilla warfare, kidnapping, theft and property destruction, the rebel groups would eventually force Shell to cease production in Ogoniland, while overall oil production would be cut by a third.

Tony was into his third rainy season when three of his fellow workers were kidnapped while out in the field repairing a pipeline which had been ruptured. One of the victims was Marcello. They'd had two guards with them, but the guards had fled, throwing away their weapons as soon as the rebels made an appearance.

The three men were freed after six weeks when the company paid the ransom demanded, but Tony decided his time in the West African country was up. Although he'd settled in well, had a Polish girlfriend, Catherine, who worked for a charity organisation, and the money was good, he'd always known it was a temporary posting.

'Shitty country, that's it for me!' Marcello fumed after his release. 'That was a bad experience. I'm not going back into the field, not here. I'll go back to Italy and find something else. Nothing is worth this.'

'Where did they keep you?'

'We moved every day, slept out in the jungle. I'm covered in fucking bites!'

'Well, I'm out too,' Tony told him. 'I've got a feeling that nothing is going to get better here for a while, and agreed: nothing is worth the risks now.'

It was nearing the end of 1988, and time to move on again.

CHAPTER TWENTY-THREE

Towards the Land of Oz

Fortunately, Tony was once again flush with money. He still had the remnants of his share from the sale of the London flat, plus a sizeable amount left over from his Colombian enterprises, both of which were boosted by savings of over £100,000 from his time in Port Harcourt. He decided therefore that time was not of the essence, and he would make his way slowly to Australia.

He flew first to Qatar, spending a couple of days on a tourist visa in the city state, where he tried his luck surfing on sand dunes without much success. There seemed little point in popping into Iran or Afghanistan, so he next flew to India, landing in Delhi and going first to take in the Taj Mahal on the banks of the River Yamuna, an hour and a half away by road.

He paid the exorbitant tourist entry fee, noticing that it was roughly ten times the amount an Indian would pay, and spent a couple of hours wandering the immaculate gardens. He had to admit it was impressive, even if the gleaming marble was no longer gleaming thanks to the pollution from nearby factories, and he didn't linger inside the burial chamber where everyone had to go barefoot because he found the stench of unwashed feet off putting. Above all, he was struggling with the crowds, something he would soon learn was a permanent feature of India. But the Taj was worth a visit, even if he didn't think it was on a par with Machu Picchu.

He stayed in Delhi two more days before the crowds and the mad traffic drove him out. He couldn't walk down the road without a horde of children following him asking for money, and he found the most distressing aspect of the hordes of humanity was the fact that the locals didn't seem to have any concept of personal space.

When he queued to get a train ticket to take him to Varanasi he had to keep pushing the man behind him away, but every time he found he was being pressed up against once more; he was sure he could even feel the man's cock.

He knew India was supposed to be a spiritual experience, and there were a good few holy men wandering around, and sacred cows dozing in the middle of the roads while the taxis and tuk-tuks swerved around them, but he wasn't feeling it. Hopefully Varanasi would be better.

He arrived after an eleven-hour journey on an overcrowded train. His fellow passengers were a friendly lot, asking him non-stop questions and plying him with food, but he wasn't really in the mood; he feigned sleep for much of the time, dreaming of the magnificent solitude and clean air of Tierradentro, which now seemed to have been from another lifetime. Every time they pulled into a station the other passengers rushed to close the windows and lock the doors to prevent even more people boarding, so pretty soon even the roof was full.

Lying on the banks of the River Ganges, Varanasi was one of the oldest continuously inhabited cities in the world, considered the cultural capital of India and venerated as a holy city. Tony checked into a quaint hotel in an early Victorian building called the Surya Kaiser Palace, about two miles from the centre of the city. The hotel only boasted eight guest rooms and was surrounded by fields and orchards, giving some respite from the bustling city, although it would later be renovated to become a luxury destination.

He rose very early the first day and took a rickshaw to the Ganges, where he hired a small boat. He rowed slowly along the miles of ghats, or steps, along the river, watching thousands of people lining up to submerge themselves in the holy water, although it looked pretty filthy to him and he wasn't sure his immune system would cope with a dip. Some sat cross-legged on the ghats, covered from head to toe in the brown mud from the river bed, lost in meditation.

But the most interesting for him was the Manikarnika Ghat, a sacred ceremonial site carrying out cremations 24/7 with an eternal flame. A tourist brochure told him it was every Hindu's greatest wish to be cremated here after death, and he could see a queue of shrouds on stretchers awaiting their turn. A pall of smoke rose from the four or five bodies already being burned on the log fire; a pair of charred feet, twisted and black, stuck out from one end of the fire, until an attendant pushed them back into the flames with a long bamboo pole, watched over by three mournful holy cows essential to the ceremony. Afterwards, the ashes and any surviving bones were thrown into the river to join the flotsam already in there.

In the afternoon, Tony wandered around the countless maze-like alleys, passing ancient astrologers, palmists and street dentists with their awesome arrays of instruments – pliers, files, knives and plastic dentures – and visiting Buddhist and Hindu temples, which were all thronged by beggars.

On the second morning he made the mistake of trying some of the delicious-looking street foods with exotic names like jalebi kachori, a kind of deep-fried bread with crispy sweetmeats, chaat, a sweet or salty crunchy pastry similar to samosas, and golgappa, a wheat flour bread stuffed with chickpeas and boiled potatoes. The rest of the day he spent in his room vomiting his guts out and sitting on the toilet with chronic diarrhoea.

Thankfully, it was just a twenty-four-hour bout of food poisoning, but once he'd recovered, he decided he'd 'done' Varanasi. In fact, he was done with India as a whole and it was time to move on again, this time by catching a flight to Kathmandu. As they descended into Kathmandu Valley in bright sunshine, Tony was almost blinded by the sparkling white view of the Himalayas, which rose majestically into the sky as far as they eye could see, and he was sure he'd made the right decision.

He checked into a cosy guest house on Jhochhen Tole in the centre of the city, an area still known as Old Freak Street from the days when its hash shops were popular with the hippies who flocked there in the 1960s, until President Nixon forced the

Nepalese government to close them down as part of his war on drugs the following decade.

Kathmandu was still a busy city, but it wasn't in the same league as India; it was more like 'India light' from Tony's perspective. No one bothered him in the streets, and he felt safe as he wandered around visiting pagodas and Buddhist and Hindu temples.

He hired a bicycle and cycled the seventeen-odd miles to the Nagarkot Tower, which was a hard journey, given that it was a climb of another 2,500 feet, Nagarkot standing at 7,000 feet. But it was worth it for the incredible mountain views – he even managed to make out Mount Everest in the distance – and the ride back was easy, being almost all downhill.

He took a bus to a village just outside Pokhara in the centre of the country, where he spent a couple of days wandering in the pure air of the foothills of the Annapurna range, until on the third day he awoke to find that a party of thirty German trekkers on an organised tour had parked their two rows of neat orange tents on the village green, which he took as a sign that it was time to move on again.

Thailand was next, and he fell in love with the place almost as soon as his flight had touched down in Bangkok. Even the airport felt welcoming, festooned with orchids and with polite immigration officers, but outside the traffic was insane, possibly the worst Tony had seen in any city. Finally, his taxi inched its way into the city centre and dropped him outside a fairly decent hotel in the main thoroughfare of Sukhumvit, where he stepped into the air-conditioned calm with a sigh of relief.

When he went out for a stroll in the evening, no one bothered him. He could see there was plenty of poverty, but also a good number of the mega-rich, and they seemed to rub along just fine. The cool young Buddhist monks in their saffron robes and sunglasses were an additional bonus.

Sukhumvit was a congested road, but numerous small streets and alleys ran off it, packed with food stalls, restaurants, bars and shops. Tony sampled his first Singha beer, and then his first plate of pad Thai: stir-fried noodles with a sweet and savoury sauce, king prawns and crushed peanuts. Then he had another beer, and thought how very happy he was to have left India behind.

After several days taking in the gleaming temples and attractions like the golden reclining Buddha at Wat Pho (all fifty yards of him), the floating markets, the Grand Palace and the seedy nightclubs around Patpong, he took a bus sixty miles east to the beach at Pattaya. Once a sleepy fishing village, it had been transformed by American GIs on R&R from Vietnam in the sixties into a fleshpot which made even Patpong seem upmarket.

Tony decided to head to an island to spend Christmas and see in the New Year, and chose Ko Chang: Elephant Island. Nearly 200 miles east of Bangkok, it was more remote and rugged than the larger and more popular tourist islands of Ko Samui and Phuket, and boasted jungle-covered mountain peaks, sweeping bays with golden sand, waterfalls and coral reefs.

Tony rented a modest beach hut to stay in. There was no air conditioning, just a large ceiling fan and the sea breeze, but the bed was comfortable and there was a shower in the bathroom. He prepared to kick back and relax for a couple of weeks, and watch the world go by.

Christmas came and went quietly; it wasn't a religious holiday for Thais, of course, although they rarely let an excuse for a party pass them by. The New Year was more raucous, with a big party at one of the beach bars. At midnight the locals released hundreds of paper lanterns into the sky, each one bearing a message of hope. Tony watched mesmerised as they floated up until they were no more than tiny pinpricks of lights, and finally disappeared.

In the end he stayed on Ko Chang for more than a month; it was a place where time seemed to stand still and he didn't notice the days passing. It was also so cheap he reckoned he could afford to stay there for another twenty years if he wanted, but he wasn't convinced that was a good plan.

He did a scuba diving course and passed his PADI Open Water test within a couple of weeks, and made half a dozen more dives before leaving. He discovered he loved the sport. Once underwater he was in a different world, silent except for when a boat passed overhead and the sound of his own breathing. He saw all manner of fish he didn't know the names of swimming over the colourful coral reefs, even some sharks, but just relatively harmless blacktips and whitetips. After each dive he would sit with the dive master and try to remember everything he had seen and put names to them while he filled up his log book. Perhaps his favourite discovery was when they saw a couple of sea horses one day, so tiny and delicate, floating among the reeds, that if they hadn't been pointed out to him by a dive 'buddy' he would never have noticed them. Afterwards, he would treat himself to a massage or manicure before dinner.

Eventually, though, he dragged himself back to the mainland and headed north to spend some time hill walking among indigenous tribes above Chiang Mai, near the border with what was then still Burma but would soon become Myanmar, although the United States refused to call it that and stuck with Burma. The villagers were friendly enough, but the area was fraught with danger too because of drug wars and ethnic groups like the Christian Karen fighting for autonomy or even independence from Rangoon, or Yangon, as some called it. 'Why do they keep fucking around with all the names?' Tony mused.

He returned to Bangkok early in April. The weather was hot, very hot, and the city was stifling. As he prepared to leave and take a train south to Malaysia and Singapore, he was caught unawares one morning when he emerged from his hotel to be drenched by someone throwing a bucket of water over him.

'What the fucking hell?' he shouted, then stopped short when he saw that everyone around him was laughing and throwing water at each other and everyone else. It was Songkran, the Thai New Year when the sun entered the astrological sign of Aries, marked by sprinkling water on statues of Buddha, honouring the elderly, and most of all by massive water fights in the streets. Tony shrugged and thought about joining in, but then the water being thrown didn't look very clean, so he retraced his steps and went back to his room to change and wait for things to calm down.

Two days later, he was on the slow train to Hat Yai, the sprawling southern town near the border with Malaysia. He had decided to spurn air travel for the rest of his journey, as he found it too disorientating to be scooped up from one culture and dumped into quite another all within the space of a few hours.

A four-hour bus ride from Hat Yai, past endless rubber tree plantations, the white sap from the trees dripping into cups tied to the trunks, and charming stilted houses next door to large modern homes with a definite British element to the architecture, delivered him to George Town on the island of Penang, the 'Pearl of the Orient', on Malaysia's northwest coast. It was a busy city, a major commercial centre with a large ethnic Chinese population, once the home of numerous opium dens long since closed down. It looked an interesting place, but Tony was only stopping one night on his way south.

He checked into a small hotel and wandered into 'Little India' in the centre of old George Town, where he ate a masala dosa, a kind of fermented rice pancake stuffed with potato curry and one of the few Indian foods he really liked, before moving to the waterfront for a nightcap. As he watched people going about their business, he couldn't help noticing that all the police seemed to be Malays, while the Chinese were the money people, and the Indians seemed mostly relegated to the more menial jobs.

He awoke early and refreshed, and, after grabbing a quick breakfast of mee goreng and a cup of coffee, he headed to the bus terminal and bought a ticket to Malacca, which was close to the causeway connecting the mainland to Singapore. He thought he'd spend one night in Malacca and make the crossing in the morning, as he didn't fancy arriving in Singapore late at night, and it was twelve hours by road. As it happened, Malacca was a small but pleasant town, and he had time to enjoy a plate of fried oysters before turning in for the night again.

Many people had told him that Singapore was a dull and boring place, clinical to the point of being antiseptic, with an oppressive regime and almost no crime. Most of which sounded quite good to him. He arrived at the border mid-morning, and although there were a few signs around warning that men with long hair would not be admitted, and would be served last in any public buildings, and the warning signs about littering threatened enormous fines, he found the officials perfectly polite and correct, and he was waved through with a minimum of fuss.

He had set his heart on spoiling himself with a stay at the iconic Raffles Hotel, but the taxi driver told him it was closed for renovation and instead recommended the Goodwood Park Hotel between Little India (there always seemed to be a Little India) and Tanglin. And that was another thing: the taxi drivers were honest!

The Goodwood Park turned out to be a good choice for the three days Tony intended to stay in Singapore before he was due to board his boat for Fremantle on Australia's west coast. The architecture was Germanic, which was hardly surprising as it had been built at the beginning of the twentieth century to serve the German expatriate community, and it boasted two swimming pools as well as one of the longest bars Tony had seen, a full forty-five feet.

He spent the next two days walking around the Botanic Gardens at Tanglin, visiting the Tiger Balm Gardens with their Ten Courts of Hell, and enjoying the restaurants and nightlife at Clarke and Boat Quay. There was also a letter from Roberto at the poste restante, which told Tony his friend had qualified as a lawyer and was now engaged to be married, and asked him to come back to Brazil to be best man at the wedding in six months' time.

Overall, Tony felt Singapore was a place he could easily live in, but on the third day he packed his bag again and headed for the port to board his ship.

CHAPTER TWENTY-FOUR

Iron Man

Tony had his own cabin on the ship, which was a blessing, as he felt little in common with the other passengers. They were mostly Brits and Australians, the former looking to work down under, the latter returning from their round-the-world adventures which had become de rigueur for the young of Australia and New Zealand before they settled down and got jobs and spouses.

Over the next eight days at sea, Tony did become friends with four Kiwis whom he dubbed 'the Wild Bunch'. Jim was the eldest at twenty-nine, then Steve, Pat, and the baby of the group, Dan, just twenty-one. They seemed to have an insatiable appetite to live life for the moment, and, although often drunk like many of the other passengers, they were funny and helped pass the time as they drifted across the ocean, past Indonesia and down along the western coast of Australia until they reached Fremantle.

Steve and Jim were subjected to full body searches, but none of them had anything illegal, and then an hour on a bus delivered them to downtown Perth, capital of Western Australia, a big sprawling city with a distinctly English flavour blessed with a hot, dry climate and plenty of sunshine. The four Kiwis rented an unfurnished house in the suburb of Leederville, about two miles from the city centre, while Tony checked into a guest house. He went to visit them the next day and found them sitting on the floor, with sleeping bags spread out in the bedrooms.

'You're going to stay here like this with no furniture?' he asked.

'Not staying long, mate,' Jim told him. 'Just waiting for some money from home, and then we're off. What about you?'

'I was thinking to get a job in one of the mines up north. Good money, apparently.'

'Good fucking luck with that, mate. Sounds like too much hard work for me. Anyway, I've been away for nearly two years; I want to go home. You should come to NZ.'

'Maybe I will once I replenish my funds.'

They went to the city beach, miles of golden sand lapped by the warm waters of the Indian Ocean, where they ogled the hundreds of tanned, blonde women in skimpy bikinis.

'Bloody hell, I could get used to this,' Steve muttered.

'Swim, anyone?' Tony suggested.

'Too many sharks, mate.'

'But there's loads of people in the water!'

'Yeah, and every now and then one gets eaten. You go, mate, we'll settle for a cold beer or two.'

Tony hesitated, then shrugged and followed them to a nearby bar. The sea around Perth did have a reputation for sharks. In fact, the sea around the whole country seemed to be teeming with them.

The next day Tony went to the recruitment offices for the iron ore mines hundreds of miles north of Perth. The fact that he was not disabled seemed enough of a qualification, although they did weigh him for some reason and he was told he was borderline underweight. He was told to eat plenty of steak and chips for the next couple of days, and report back for his flight to Mount Tom Price three days later. He signed up for the minimum six months.

After saying his farewells to the Kiwis, who were still waiting for funds, he duly reported back to the recruitment offices three days later and was flown the 650 miles up to Mount Tom Price, along with a couple of dozen other new recruits.

The isolated township stood amidst a stunning but harsh landscape, desert scrubland and the mountains of the Hamersley range, which were so full of iron ore they were said to rust in the rain. On arrival, Tony was given a pair of steel-toed work boots, two pairs of overalls and a green plastic hard hat, and allocated a room in one of the long, prefabricated cabins which housed the more than 2,000 single men. There were also around a hundred houses for married workers.

The room itself was small, with bare walls, a wonky desk and chair, a cracked mirror and a metal wardrobe. It was clearly designed for sleeping only. Tony sat down at the wobbly desk and composed a letter back to Roberto, giving him his news and saying that he couldn't promise to be in Brazil within six months for the wedding, but would try to come later.

After mailing it, he went to the twenty-four-hour canteen, where he made the mistake of ordering a steak which was as tough as shoe leather, accompanied by some potatoes and carrots that had been boiled to death. Dessert was some sort of stodgy pudding covered by watery custard, after which Tony staggered back to his cell feeling like he'd swallowed a couple of lead weights.

The next morning, he was told he was to work as a fitter's mate and assigned to a 'gang'. They were a motley group: Vic the lead hand with half-tied boots and a thick Hungarian accent, Les the Tasmanian with no front teeth, Alf the Swede whose every other word was 'fucking', Billy the boilermaker, a short rotund man from Queensland, and Bob, a muscular young man from New South Wales who was the only married man amongst them. They were easy going and unassuming people, and they gave Tony a warm welcome and showed him the ropes. His job was basically to accompany one of the fitters on any given job, carry his tools, hand the relevant tool to him as requested, and clean up afterwards. He felt a bit like a surgeon's assistant, except, instead of 'scalpel' being called out, it was 'wrench' or 'hammer'.

It was dusty, dirty work, so there were frequent stops to take on water with salt tablets, and have a smoke, unless one of the 'white hats', the senior engineers, were in the vicinity. As far as possible, they worked slowly so there would be plenty of overtime, repairing diggers or trucks.

The worst part was when one of them had to don a plastic suit from head to toe and enter the oil well of one of the diggers, which was invariably Tony's job as the junior; it meant literally swimming around in the oil in near-boiling temperatures, while trying to follow shouted instructions.

The mine was an ugly scar on the landscape. They were literally dynamiting the mountains and then scraping the iron ore off, and loading it into huge dump trucks, which then took it to the railyard to be sent to the coast for export, mostly to China.

For the first two weeks Tony worked sixteen hours a day without a break. At breakfast the canteen also supplied a packed lunch, and it was still open for the night shift when he returned to the town.

After that first fortnight, though, he had begun making some friends and insisted on taking one day a week off, and working shorter hours. Most of the extra time he had on his hands was spent in the town's only pub, playing darts and placing bets on horse races. He'd never been a betting man before, but one of his new friends, Mike, introduced him to the horses, claiming he had a cast-iron system which guaranteed they couldn't lose.

'No such thing,' Tony told him. 'If there was, the bookies would out of business overnight.'

'I tell you, man, you can't lose; you just have to hold your nerve,' Mike retorted. He was a large man from the Blue Mountains with a huge bushy black beard, oddly small delicate hands, and an intoxicating laugh.

'Explain it to me, then.'

'Okay, well, we each stump up $1,000 to put in the pot. Then we start small, say with bets of twenty or a maximum fifty dollars. Every time we win, the money goes into the pot.'

'And if we lose?' Tony poured himself another glass of beer from the jug they were sharing.

'Ah, now there's the trick,' Mike explained, running a hand through his beard. 'If we lose, let's say on a twenty-dollar bet, then on the next race we double our bet to forty dollars. Then, if we lose again, we go in at eighty dollars. Sooner or later, we're bound to win again, and, if we double our money each time we lose, it means we'll be guaranteed to get back all our losses.'

'Sounds a bit too good to be true,' Tony mused. 'But then I'll give it a go, just to relieve some of the boredom of this place. Let's start with $500 each and see how it goes.'

For a couple of months, the system seemed to work, and they had nearly doubled their original stake. But then they went on a serious losing streak which not only emptied their pot but left them staring at making a bet of $1,000 on a single race, and if that lost then the next bet would be $2,000.

'It was good while it lasted,' Tony decided, 'but I'm out.'

'Yeah, guess you're right,' Mike agreed. 'Otherwise, if we keep losing, we'll be stuck working in this shithole forever.'

And getting stuck in Mount Tom Price ad infinitum was definitely not part of the plan, Tony thought. The work was repetitive: wake up, eat breakfast, work, smoke, work, lunch, work, smoke, work, tea, and then usually some overtime because there was nothing much else to do, even though he'd invested in a small cross-country motorbike and spent the odd day motoring around the desert with a few other riders. Occasionally they'd chance upon a small waterfall in one of the gorges, and his mind would drift back to the Amazon.

He'd also managed to get his HGV driving licence, and had been taken off the fitters' team and given a Hiab truck to drive, a lorry with a mounted hydraulic crane on the back and a set of levers to move it around. Not only was he paid more, but it was a lot more fun driving from one part of the mine to the other, lifting engines and other parts for repair.

Halfway through his time at the mine he'd already recouped the money he'd spent while travelling, and was beginning to think of his next move.

A day after his six months were completed, he collected his new pair of company boots. Everyone was entitled to a new pair each six months, and he had grown to like them; they were suede and just above ankle height, and those steel toecaps were an added bonus. A week later he handed in his notice and was flown back to Perth.

CHAPTER TWENTY-FIVE

Rondônia Revisited

Roberto had written to say his wedding had been postponed for three months until February, and Tony had told him he would be there in time to see in the new decade. He didn't stay in Perth, but boarded the Indian Pacific trans-Australian train to Sydney and spent three days watching the vast country move slowly by. He loved train journeys, and this was one of the best – not as long as the trans-Siberian, at just over 2,700 miles, but a lot more comfortable.

For the first day they moved through mostly desert scrubland with little sign of life, and at night he slept soundly to the sound of the wheels trundling along the tracks. They skirted the Coober Pedy opal fields and arrived in Adelaide late on the second day, by which time the landscape had turned green. Then it was through Broken Hill and the Blue Mountains, and into Sydney on the Pacific coast.

It looked an interesting city, but Tony was in a hurry now. Moving had become almost an end in itself; he was restless after spending six months in the confines of Mount Tom Price, and, after a couple of days visiting various travel agents, he came across the perfect deal. The deal offered to take him from Sydney to London, travelling east with as many as six stops, to be completed within a year. It wasn't cheap, but he seemed to be awash with money anyway and was happy to spend some of it on something that fitted his plans. While he wanted to get back to Brazil, he also felt the time was coming when he needed to go home again. He was coming full circle in his search for peace of mind and the meaning of life, if there was one.

He flew first to Auckland with Quantas, an experience which

made him understand why it was dubbed 'Cute Ass' when a steward plied him with wine and invited him out for dinner in New Zealand, an invitation he politely declined. Auckland seemed a bit of a hick town, mostly low-rise with lots of timber-framed houses and endless suburbs, and an unimpressive main thoroughfare called Queen Street, which boasted more than its fair share of drunken Māori men who didn't look the kind of people you'd want to tangle with.

Tony tracked down the 'Wild Bunch' – Jim had given him his parents' address – whom he found sharing a large house in the suburbs, all of them working on building sites. Waking with a monumental hangover after a night on the tiles with them, he made his way back to the airport and boarded a LAN Chile flight to Santiago de Chile, where he arrived a day earlier than he had left thanks to crossing the international date line.

The Chilean capital was an impressive place. The taxi driver who took him downtown from the airport wore white gloves, and the car had a meter, something Tony had never encountered in his time in Colombia.

'You know, we are the English of South America,' the driver said when Tony told him where he was from. 'We like to think the English are our special friends.'

'You certainly helped us in the Falklands War... or should I say Islas Malvinas?'

'We speak Spanish, so most people would say Islas Malvinas, but either is okay. In fact, a lot of us say "las Islas Falklands", just to annoy the Argentinians. You know, I am from Valparaiso, and there is an Anglican church there with an organ donated by Queen Victoria after an earthquake. You should go and see it.'

'I'd like to, but I don't have the time. I have to go to Brazil for a wedding.'

He was dropped off in Barrio Italia and checked into a cosy guest house, then spent the next couple of days exploring the city. He took the funicular up San Cristóbal Hill, at the top of which there were panoramic views and a huge statue of the Virgin Mary, and spent hours in the huge Central Market, which was apparently inspired by London's Billingsgate fish market, with the cast iron roof having been made in Glasgow and shipped out to Chile. Nearby there was a mini copy of Big Ben in the street, and best of all, around the corner from where he was staying, he discovered the best hamburger bar he'd ever been in anywhere in the world. The staff worked inside the huge circular bar, so you could watch while sipping on a large tankard of fresh beer as they prepared your food, but getting a place to sit wasn't easy and tended to involve queuing behind someone and waiting until they vacated their seat.

A couple of days before Christmas, Tony managed to get a seat on a LAN Chile flight to Rio de Janeiro, where he picked up a local connecting flight to Porto Alegre. Roberto was waiting for him in the arrivals hall with a huge grin and bear hug. 'Man, you get around! Africa, Asia, Australia, the A-list! Come, we have a lot to talk about, but first a cold beer maybe?'

'Sounds about right to me,' Tony said. 'Lead the way.'

Roberto had a spacious apartment in the neighbourhood of Moinhos de Vento, near the historic old centre of the city, which boasted older buildings and an abundance of wooded parkland. The streets were festooned with Christmas lights, crowds were out shopping, and, being summer, the evening was very warm.

'I have to thank you for coming; it means a lot to me,' Roberto said once they were sitting at a table outside a bar, with two ice cold Brahma Chopp beers in front of them.

'I'm very happy to be here,' Tony told him. 'Lucky for me that you postponed the wedding – why was that, by the way?'

'My mother was very ill; she's okay now. She lives not far from here. We'll see her tomorrow for our Christmas dinner – here the main meal is in the evening on the twenty-fourth. But anyway, I'm glad we delayed. It's better to get Christmas over, then we can have a nice honeymoon after the wedding.'

'And where is your good lady?'

'Juliana? She is with her family in Torres. It's by the sea, not so far.'

'She doesn't live in Porto Alegre, then?'

'Oh, yes, she's a doctor here. You will meet her just after Christmas. I'm sure you'll like her. At least I hope so!'

'Of course I will, look forward to it.'

'And there's something else. I have a surprise for you, for after the New Year.'

'A surprise?'

'I have tickets for us both to go to Porto Velho. I still have a few things to tie up there, and anyway I wanted to see the old farm one last time. See what happened to it, think of it as a trip down memory lane.'

'Oh, wow! Are you serious? That sounds amazing, it'll be really interesting. I'll pay you for my tickets.'

'No way, it's my present. You've done enough just by being here, all the way from the other side of the world!'

They spent a quiet Christmas dinner with Roberto's elderly mother Fernanda, and on Christmas Day itself went for a long walk along the banks of the giant freshwater lake, the Lagoa dos Patos, which was big enough for oceangoing ships to navigate.

'A shame Senice isn't still here,' Roberto mused.

'When did he pass away?'

'Just over a year ago; he contracted hardpad.'

'Sorry to hear that. He was a lovely dog.'

New Year was a rowdier affair, and they were joined by Juliana, some fifteen years younger than Roberto, a slim blonde woman with green eyes, which she explained by saying her grandparents had been German.

'They came after the war?' Tony couldn't resist asking.

'Actually, just before,' she told him. 'They were escaping the Nazis. A lot of Germans settled in Rio Grande do Sul.'

They watched the municipal fireworks together and drank champagne, and sat up late talking and playing music from Roberto's collection of old vinyl records. Three days later, Roberto and Tony flew to Porto Velho.

The rain was lashing down as they landed in Porto Velho; the rainy season was in full swing. Instead of the dusty, sleepy town Tony had first encountered more than ten years earlier, he was confronted with a huge sprawling city of almost 300,000 people, surrounded by shanty towns. Rondônia in general, and Porto Velho in particular, had been one of the biggest magnets for migrants in Amazonia, with thousands upon thousands of people drawn to the promise of riches in the cassiterite mines, the timber trade, what was left of the rubber business, and, most importantly of all, agriculture and cattle farming. And still they were coming.

Roberto had a hire car waiting for them, a Suzuki jeep, and they drove into town through half-flooded streets and checked into the Hotel Central. Tony dumped his bag in his room, which was basic but clean at least, and with air conditioning, then went to the bar. Roberto, meanwhile, headed off to see his lawyer to settle some outstanding affairs from the sale of the farm and collect some money which was still owed to him.

The following day the rain had eased, and they drove out to what had been Water Flower Garden. The jungle had been cleared back from both sides of the road for several hundred yards, replaced by red scrubland where the soil had been washed away.

'Christ, what a clusterfuck,' Tony muttered, looking at the devastation.

'Around twenty-five percent of the forest in Rondônia has been cleared already,' Roberto told him as he struggled to keep the small jeep straight on the slippery road surface. 'Part of it is mining, but the biggest culprit is cattle farming.'

'It's depressing.'

'For sure, and it's one of the reasons I decided to chuck it in. The deforestation increases greenhouse gas emissions, while at the same time reducing the carbon sink effects of the jungle. They're also killing the biodiversity of the forest. If they carry on like this, one day it'll be more like a desert than a forest.'

When they drew up at the old farm, they could see that their precious orange grove had disappeared. In its place, on both sides of the road, were hundreds and hundreds of fenced-in scrawny zebu cattle foraging for food.

'Let's go see the waterfall, maybe have a swim?' Tony suggested.

'We can try. We'd better ask.'

They drove into the farm. The old house was still there, and Tony's, even though the yellow paint had faded and peeled and green mould was creeping up the walls. Apart from the cattle, the whole place had a neglected feel about it.

As they stopped, a farmhand approached and asked their business, but once they'd explained who they were and said they just wanted to look around and walk to the waterfall, they were told it was no problem as long as they didn't bother the cattle.

The old path through the jungle wasn't there any more, because the jungle wasn't. They walked across newly cleared fields all the way, and then stared in disbelief at their old secret paradise. The waterfall was still there, but the vegetation around the pool had all been cleared and the ground at the edges of the water had been trampled by thousands of hooves.

'I'm not swimming in that,' Tony said gloomily. 'Come on, we've seen enough. Let's go, because this place is getting me down.'

As they walked back to the jeep, the heavens opened again and the rain came crashing down, soaking them to the skin within a few yards.

'Maybe coming up here was a mistake,' Roberto suggested as they drove back to Porto Velho.

'No, I'm glad we came; now I won't dream of it any more. It was beautiful, but not now. I won't be coming back anyway!'

'I can't believe what they are doing to the place.'

'The world is going to hell in a handcart, my friend.'

The rain didn't stop as they ate dinner in a halfway decent steakhouse that evening. 'Meat around here is still tough as old boots,' Tony remarked, chewing. 'We never did get to build that abattoir.'

'And now we never will.'

In the end it was a relief when they checked out and flew back to Porto Alegre.

CHAPTER TWENTY-SIX

HOMECOMING

The wedding was held in Juliana's hometown of Torres. It was secular and held in a large marquee erected on a clifftop overlooking the Atlantic Ocean. Juliana was stunning in a long, dark green silk dress, while Roberto was in a white suit and Tony in one of midnight blue.

The weather was perfect, blue skies and the temperature in the low twenties Celsius. Once the vows were made and the rings exchanged, a sumptuous meal was laid on with a live band, and the dancing continued late into the night.

Tony was happy for his friend, but sad to see him leave the next morning as he and Juliana departed for their honeymoon in Fernando de Noronha, an archipelago of islands a couple of hundred miles off the country's northeast coast. They said he could stay in his hotel, and he did for a couple of days, enjoying the beaches and the sea, but soon his mind was turning to the reality of having to return to England.

His flight touched down at London's Heathrow airport on a miserable day in the middle of February, the rain pelting down from a leaden sky. After clearing customs, he took the underground into town, changing at Earl's Court to pick up the District Line south to Wimbledon Park, where he would stay with friends until he had sorted himself out.

His first priority the next day was to head to the benefits office to sign on, so he could enjoy spending other people's money while pretending to look for a job. Half the country seemed to be doing it from what he could work out, so he thought he might as well join the scam. Most of the rest of the day he spent in the pub enjoying his first few pints of good English bitter for many years, and with the Young's brewery just around the corner it was very good.

He flicked through the local newspaper's classified advertisements searching for a suitable car, and his eye caught the section dealing with camper vans. *Yes!* he thought. *That's it!* It was a lightbulb moment: until he had decided on a more long-term plan, he would live in a camper van and tour the country, which was something he'd never done, despite travelling around half the world. It would get him out of his friends' house, where he knew the two small children would soon drive him up the wall, and, just as importantly, it would get him out of London. Already the city felt different from the one he had left behind: it was shabbier and incredibly expensive, people seemed downtrodden, and in the streets few of the people actually seemed to be English any more.

On his way back to the terraced Victorian house which his friends owned, he picked up a copy of *AutoTrader*, and he spent the evening thumbing through the advertisements and making notes.

'You could try looking on the internet,' his mate James suggested.

'No, he can't,' his wife Sally interrupted. 'I'm waiting for a phone call.'

'I've not got into the internet thing yet,' Tony told them. 'I mean, the dial-up is so slow. I prefer the old-fashioned way.'

Eventually he settled on a black second-hand Mercedes light commercial vehicle with relatively low mileage, which he would convert himself. 'I mean, how difficult can it be?' he asked. 'Just need someone to cut a window in the side, then I can build the rest myself.'

It took him a month, but he was well pleased with the result. A large privacy window was duly cut on the side opposite the sliding door, along with another small one in the roof, then he insulated the inside with foam and plywood, and built a generous single bed with drawers underneath, a small wardrobe, and installed a pump action sink which drained straight outside, and a chemical toilet. For cooking he had decided to rely on a gas Primus stove, while he also fitted a shower attachment which could be used outside, weather permitting. Finally, in the third week of March he set off, heading up the east coast, aiming to eventually visit a cousin in Aberdeen.

His first stop was Aldeburgh on the Suffolk coast, a pretty enough place, but as it was pre-Easter more than half the houses were still empty, awaiting their north London owners who filled the place up during the holiday seasons. But it did boast a couple of good fish and chip shops, along with pubs serving delicious nutty Adnams beers brewed in nearby Southwold, and, best of all, public conveniences where he could wash and shave in comfort. The North Sea, however, looked grey and uninviting, and the wind whipping in was cold, so after a couple of nights in a layby he decided to push on.

For the next two weeks he pushed slowly up the east coast, sampling the beers and taking in the best sights. Through Norfolk, where he kept an eye out for people with six fingers, to Lincolnshire, which was as flat as a pancake, even if the cathedral in Lincoln City was truly awe-inspiring. In Yorkshire he decided to take a look at Hull, which on the map looked like the kind of place you would have to go to deliberately; lying on the River Hull at its confluence with the Humber Estuary, it wasn't on the way to anywhere else, and apparently not many visitors seemed to go out of their way to take in whatever it had to offer. He was soon to find out why.

Hull, or more correctly Kingston upon Hull, was the second most bombed city in Britain after London in World War Two, with ninety-five percent of its buildings damaged or destroyed. Since then, it had suffered post-industrial decline and social deprivation, and, more recently, its once-great fishing industry had been destroyed by EU quotas.

Tony drove past drab 1960s concrete tower blocks on the outskirts, along with a surprising number of back-to-back terraced houses which had somehow survived, many of them still with concrete air raid shelters in their back gardens. But, despite the general air of being down at heel, the Old Town was a pleasant surprise, with its cobbled streets, shops, restaurants and pubs, in which he found good local beers and very friendly locals. There were also some magnificent old buildings, among them the Wilberforce House Museum, former home of William Wilberforce who led the campaign to end slavery in the late eighteenth and early nineteenth centuries, and the Beverley Minster was nearby. Tony parked up near the city's marina, and spent three nights and two very pleasant days there, but he still felt lost with no idea where his life was heading.

From Yorkshire he drove to Durham for a look at the stunning cathedral there, then on to Northumberland, skirting Sunderland and stopping in Newcastle for a couple of days. Despite the sun making an appearance between the few clouds scudding across the sky, it was still cold, but that didn't seem to trouble the Geordies, many of whom wandered about in T-shirts and shorts, while the young women sported the shortest of skirts and skimpy tops, their legs bare. It was enough to make Tony shiver and pull his fleece jacket tighter.

He struggled to understand many of the locals with their strong accents, but, while in the pubs they joked that he was a southern 'poofter', they were friendly enough and good company. The city centre itself was impressive, especially the historic Grainger Town with its multitude of shops, bars and cafés, even if there seemed to be a Greggs sausage roll and pastry shop on every other corner, this being the original home of the chain, and the outskirts promised little in the way of attractions.

Fifty miles further north, Tony paid a visit to Bamburgh Castle, a site which had been lived on for thousands of years, and which Anglo-Saxon kings in Northumbria had chosen as their capital, with its natural harbour and easily defended escarpment towering 150 feet above the North Sea. As he wandered the remains and inside the restored areas, he tried to imagine how it had been in ancient times, remembering novels he had read about the struggles between Vikings from Denmark, the Anglo-Saxons and the original Britons, and once again he marvelled at the history of his homeland, as well as the surprisingly beautiful vistas it still offered, despite its relatively small size.

He crossed into the Scottish borderlands and headed for Edinburgh, where he parked up at Portobello Beach, a couple of miles from the city centre, and booked into the old Victorian Turkish baths for a session the following day. He caught a bus back to the city, and, after wandering around the labyrinthine alleys of the Old Town, he decided to climb Arthur's Seat, an extinct volcano about 800 feet tall in the middle of Holyrood Park, which offered superb panoramic views of Edinburgh. Quite why it was called Arthur's Seat, no one seemed exactly sure; it seemed unlikely that the legendary King Arthur ever made it to the city, although one tour guide told Tony a story about the volcano having once been a dragon which had fallen asleep and never woken up again, which also seemed a bit unlikely.

The climb had made Tony hungry, so once back down in the city he found a café which served a huge helping of haggis, neeps and tatties: not everyone's cup of tea, but Tony had always been fond of haggis.

That night he slept soundly in Portobello Beach, listening to the wind and the waves from the North Sea, and the next morning, once breakfast was out of the way, he made his way to the Turkish baths. They represented one of the few Turkish baths left in the country, and they were wonderful. His session was for one hour and forty-five minutes; he had time to go through all three hot chambers, the tepidarium (warm), the caldarium (hot) and the laconium (hottest), and then finished it off by immersing himself in the icy cold plunge pool. The only thing missing was someone to soap and scrub him, but he still felt like a million dollars when he came out.

Shortly afterwards he was driving across the Firth of Forth towards Dundee, and a couple of hours later reached Aberdeen, often referred to as the 'silver city' on account of all the granite buildings, which are supposed to sparkle and look silvery when the sun comes out after rainfall. Unfortunately, while it rained a lot, the sun rarely made an appearance, and to Tony the granite buildings and multiple high-rise apartment blocks on the outskirts just looked grey and uninviting.

Nevertheless, the city was still enjoying the oil boom years, although they wouldn't last a lot longer, and the country had little to show for all that oil revenue, which was mostly in the hands of private companies. Margaret Thatcher had made the mistake of selling off the state-owned British National Oil Corporation, BNOC, to BP for a little over a paltry £400 million: money which, if invested in a sovereign wealth fund as the Norwegians were doing with very similar oil revenues, might have been worth £500 billion or more forty years later. Instead, it went on tax cuts, which were anyway negated when the Chancellor, Nigel Lawson, increased VAT rates.

Tony passed by the port, but it was quiet; like Hull, Aberdeen's fishing industry had been hollowed out. He drove down the main drag of Union Street and out to the suburb of Woodside, where he drew up outside his cousin Stanley's bungalow in the early afternoon.

'Tony, my boy!' Stanley exclaimed when he opened the door. He was ten years older than Tony but several inches shorter, and had developed a noticeable paunch, while his greying hair was thinning and receding, combed back off his forehead. 'Are we too early for a pint of heavy?'

'It's got to be sundown somewhere.' Tony grinned back as they gave each other a hug.

'Rarely comes up here, lad. Come on, let's get your stuff inside and then we'll go down the road.' He looked over at the Mercedes. 'Those your wheels, then?'

'That's my *home* at the moment,' Tony told him. 'Trying to work out what to do next.'

'Och, well, it's a bonny one at that, but could be a bit cold in winter.'

'Maybe something will come up before then; we'll see.' Tony shrugged and grabbed his bag, and they took it inside.

Stanley's wife, Fiona, had passed away with cancer two years earlier, and the bungalow was cluttered inside with assorted bric-abrac from various car boot sales. One room was full of old vinyl records, which were Stanley's passion.

'Oh, and there's a letter for you here,' Stanley said. 'Arrived last week, it did.'

Tony looked at the envelope. It was from Brazil, but he didn't recognise the writing. Frowning, he tore it open, and then began crying softly as he read the single page.

'Bad news, is it, lad? What's happened?'

'Yeah, it's bad news all right.'

Stanley took him by the arm and led him to a chair. 'Come on, sit down, I'll make you a cup of tea.'

The letter was from Juliana. Roberto had been in a bad car accident and was in a coma in hospital. To make matters worse, Juliana was pregnant and was asking Tony to be the godfather of their son or daughter.

'He's my best mate,' Tony said dully as he sipped the strong sweet tea. 'We went through a lot together up in the Amazon, and I was his best man at his wedding just a couple of months ago. I can't believe this is happening.'

'Aye, that's bad, right enough,' Stanley sighed. 'But God willing he'll pull through. Will you be going back out there?'

'Maybe. Not much point if he's in a coma, but I'll give Juliana a call. It'll be expensive, but I'll pay, and I won't stay on the line long.'

'Dinnae be daft, go right ahead. The telephone is in the hallway.'

Tony dialled the operator and put in a trunk call, and soon after listened to the phone ringing on the other side of the world. Juliana answered and Tony started crying again, saying how sorry he was and that of course he'd be proud to be the godfather of their child, and he'd come out when he could, and what hope was there for Roberto? She told him through her own tears that it was too early to tell; his car had been hit by a truck driving back to Porto Alegre from Torres just weeks after their honeymoon. Five minutes later, Tony quietly replaced the receiver in its cradle and just stood looking at the floor.

Stanley came into the hall. 'Come on, lad, let's get you out. We've a lot to talk about, and talking always helps. You have to tell me all about this Roberto fellow.'

Half an hour later they were sitting inside the Highlander nursing their pints and whisky chasers, while Tony poured his heart out, Stanley listening sympathetically.

'The thing is, Stan, I feel completely rudderless. I was happy in the Amazon, my life had meaning, everything made sense. And then I was happy in Colombia too. But they were both snatched away from me. Now I've no idea what to do, or what's the point of anything.'

'That's no way to think.' Stanley drained his whisky and took a gulp of beer. 'There's always a point. You might not be able to see it right now, but you will. Keep an open mind.'

'Yes, yes, I know. I just need to keep going, but this thing with Roberto has been a body blow.'

'Like I said, with luck he'll pull through, and you need to be strong. But tell you what: if you want to see hopeless, I've got a couple of tickets for the Dons tomorrow. You'll come with me?'

Tony laughed despite himself. 'Sure, that'll be fun.'

Pittodrie stadium, perched on the edge of the North Sea, had to be the coldest football ground in the country. Stanley and Tony sat and shivered in a bitter wind as they watched Aberdeen battle it out to beat Glasgow Celtic two goals to one, a rare victory against one of the giants of Scottish football. But then, Tony mused, it wasn't so long since Aberdeen, under the stewardship of Alex Ferguson, had won the European Cup Winners' Cup, and the Scottish Cup four times. Unfortunately, Ferguson had been lured south a few years back to seek his fortune with Manchester United.

A few days later Tony drove on to Inverness and stayed overnight on the shores of Loch Ness, Britain's largest volume of fresh water and home to Nessie, who of course made no appearance. He skirted Glasgow and carried on to the Lake District, home to Scafell Pike, England highest mountain at just over 3,000 feet, and a timeless tapestry of spectacular lakes and countryside. He stayed in the ancient town of Keswick at the northern end of

Derwentwater and briefly considered hiking up some of the lower and less challenging mountains, but it was raining and he decided after one night to keep going.

He was getting tired of the constant moving. Living in a van was all very well, but it was quite a lot of work too in that, as on a boat, everything had to be kept clean and tidied away all the time, and now he just wanted to reach his next target of Land's End as soon as possible. It had become his target just because he liked the sound of it.

And so it was that he trundled down through Lancashire, Cheshire and Shropshire and on to Herefordshire, giving a miss to Blackpool, Birmingham and the whole of Wales, until he reached Gloucestershire, where he stopped for the night in Stroud, a pretty town once memorably referred to as 'Notting Hill with wellies' by one London newspaper, standing below the western escarpment of the Cotswold Hills. The next day he passed through Wiltshire and Somerset and entered north Devon, and from there hugged the dramatic coast down to Cornwall, past Newquay and St Ives to Penzance and, finally, Land's End, the British mainland's most south westerly point.

CHAPTER TWENTY-SEVEN

PUTTING DOWN ROOTS

Once at Land's End, Tony parked up and entered the oddly tacky collection of buildings, which included a mini theme park, the inevitable pasty shop and other shops selling souvenirs. He walked on past Penwith House, once a temperance hotel for teetotal Victorians but now offering luxury accommodation, until he came to the famous sign which told him he was 3,147 miles from New York. After getting his photo taken, he stood at the edge of the 200-foot-high granite cliffs and breathed in the fresh North Atlantic air deeply. It was a startlingly bright day with blue skies, and in the distance, he could just make out the smudge that was the Scilly Isles, some thirty miles away.

He wandered towards the First and Last House for an ice cream, and on the way read a plaque which told him there were more than 130 recorded shipwrecks around Land's End, and many more unrecorded. On the rocks below he could make out several grey seals, and he had been told that dolphins and basking sharks were also fairly common.

He loved it: the wildness of the area, the infinite sea, the gulls whirling above screeching defiance; it felt almost as if he was in a different country. And in a way, he was. In the late eighteenth century, the writer Samuel Johnson had written a spoof about a Cornish declaration of independence, which pointed out that the people of Cornwall were the earliest inhabitants of Britain who were paying taxes to usurpers, and that they had as strong a case for independence as America, declaring the right to administer and tax themselves. It was, Johnson said, the forgotten fifth nation of the United Kingdom.

Later, sitting in the First and Last Inn in Sennen a few miles away, Tony was astonished to hear two old men chattering away in an incomprehensible language, and asked the landlord what it was.

'Oh, that? It's Kernowek,' the landlord, a dour man with an apron and a walrus moustache, told him.

'It's what?'

'Kernowek. Cornish to you. It's an ancient Celtic language.'

'Like Welsh, you mean?'

'Like Welsh in as much as they are both Celtic languages, but Cornish is different. Not that many speak it these days, but it's growing again. They're even teaching it in some of the primary schools.'

'Wow! I had no idea. Is it difficult to learn?'

'I reckon,' the landlord said, polishing a glass.

Tony decided to make his way back towards Penzance to spend the night, first stopping by at the nearby world-famous Minack open-air theatre, a spectacular Greek-inspired amphitheatre clinging to the granite rocks above Porthcurno beach. There was no play on, but he paid to go inside anyway and marvelled at the landscaped gardens and the steep terraces cut into the cliffside for the audiences, and, beyond the stage below, the shimmering sea. It was more remarkable to learn that, founded in the 1930s, it was mostly the work of one woman, Rowena Cade, who had moved to Cornwall after the death of her father in World War One, helped by her gardener friend Billy Rawlings.

The town of Penzance and its harbour sat on a stunning stretch of shoreline with a backdrop of beautiful countryside, but, while the name of the place conjured up images of pirates and glamour, the reality was a bit more depressing. It had clearly seen better times and everything looked a bit down at heel. Tony parked and walked up Market Jew Street past several boarded-up shops, a couple with young homeless men in the doorways begging from passers-by.

He had more luck in Chapel Street, where he ducked into the Admiral Benbow pub for a couple of pints of Hicks and some fish and chips, finding himself in a restaurant that was a magnificent reconstruction of a ship's deck, complete with the stern plate from a Portuguese man o' war. There were also several recovered ships' figureheads and a cannon to complete the picture.

As evening fell, he drove over to Marazion and pulled over opposite St Michael's Mount, a tidal island which had already been a harbour 2,000 years earlier. A few dozen people still lived there, overlooked by the castle at the top of the mount, and as the sun sank it made for a stunning sight. Tony was beginning to get a feel for Cornwall; the abundance of palm trees even made it feel quite exotic.

The following day he drove slowly back up the A30, past Porthia (St Ives) and Porthrepta, and turned off for Heyl. He drove through to the other side and then took the coastal road to Gwithian Towans, where he spent the afternoon watching the surfers on the huge Atlantic swell and enjoying the rugged beauty of the beach and sand dunes, golden hills tufted with wild grass alongside dramatic cliffs. He thought surfing was something he might have to investigate.

He had decided he preferred this remote corner of the county to some of the more popular towns further north, such as Padstow or Port Isaac, which were already becoming gentrified, and nor was he interested in the south coast and the English Channel. The question was where to put down some roots. Because that, he realised, was what he wanted to do.

To this end he spent the next fortnight driving up and down the coast, spending the night in a different place each time, searching for the town or village that felt just right. He didn't want to be too isolated. If necessary, he wanted to be able to walk to everything: the doctor, the dentist, the local shops, a couple of cafés or a restaurant maybe, and a pub or two. And he wanted to be as close as possible to the sea.

Eventually he settled on the village of Porthrepta, a small community, but with all the basic essentials, a few miles outside St Ives, which had felt too cramped to him, with its tiny cobbled streets which were apparently overrun with tourists in the summer season. Porthrepta was mostly built on steep cliffs overlooking a charming northeasterly-facing bay, which made for a calmer sea than the west-facing surfing ones.

Within days Tony hit gold when he found a two-bedroom cottage for sale within his budget and with sea views. He didn't bother haggling, and as a cash buyer his offer was quickly accepted. Within two months he had a new home, just a ten-minute walk away from the beach, although coming back up the steep hill took a bit longer.

He immediately wrote to Juliana with his new address, and set about putting his own stamp on the property, redecorating and buying all-new furniture and bedding. He also sold the Mercedes, and replaced it with a more economical hatchback. After his first dip in the sea, he added a wetsuit to his wardrobe.

Tony discovered that the Cornish were notoriously suspicious of outsiders, although that was something that didn't bother him as he was by now used to his own company. In time, however, he began to get involved in the local community, first by volunteering to drive elderly people to their various appointments, then by getting a job at the seal sanctuary near Helston; it didn't pay much, but then money wasn't his main concern.

He was amazed to learn that ninety-five percent of the European and forty percent of the world's population of grey seals were in British waters, and that their numbers had recovered from only 500 early in the twentieth century to more than 120,000 a century later. He enjoyed the work, which he was to discover was especially busy in the breeding season from September until March, when the Cornish sanctuary rescued dozens of seal pups who were either malnourished or separated from their mothers, and nursed them back to health before releasing them back into the wild.

A letter arrived from Juliana in June to say that, miraculously, Roberto was out of his coma, and was expected to make an almost full recovery. Her baby was due at the end of October and she wondered if there was any possibility Tony could come out for the christening. As he lay in bed that night listening to the hoots of a nearby owl, he decided that of course he would make one last trip to Brazil; how could he not?

November in Torres made for a welcome relief from the grey skies and dark days of England at that time of the year. Juliana had delivered a baby boy, who they had named Tiago, and Tony formally became the godfather at the christening ceremony. Roberto was still in a wheelchair, but was undergoing intensive physiotherapy and was looking forward to walking unaided again in the next few weeks.

In the evening, while Juliana was putting Tiago to bed, Tony and Roberto sat outside and opened a bottle of pinga for old times' sake.

'Any news from the Amazon?' Tony asked, after throwing back his shot of the fermented sugarcane and sucking on a slice of lemon.

'It's a disaster, my friend. They are still cutting and burning and mining. At this rate there will be no forest left by the time we die, and then what?'

'Whole world is fucked if you ask me. There are just too many people.'

'You know, there are more than half a million people in Porto Velho now.'

'No way! And do you know, when I was born, there were less than two and a half billion people in the world. Now it's over five and a half billion, and in another ten years they reckon it'll be more than eight billion. Imagine when it's twenty billion. It's unsustainable.'

'Poor Tiago.'

'Yeah, I wonder what the future will be like for young people in, say, 2050. Fortunately, I won't be around to see it.'

'You and me both, my friend.'

Tony stayed for a week, enjoying the sunshine and the friendship, and before he left, he made Roberto and Juliana promise that the next visit would be them coming to see him.

'I'd love that,' Juliana told him. 'I've never been to Europe.'

Back in Cornwall, Tony resumed his work at the seal sanctuary and added voluntary work at the food bank in nearby Camborne to his schedule. He hadn't realised before that the county was actually one of the poorest regions in northern Europe; the coastal tourist spots tended to disguise much of the poverty, but visits to places like Camborne, Pool and Redruth were enough to see how desperate some people were in the old tin mining areas in the centre of Cornwall, where there was real deprivation. The Camborne food bank alone was supporting some 500 families, and each year it was getting worse.

For Christmas, he acquired a companion in the shape of a Patterdale terrier, a small but very robust black dog who needed a firm hand at first, but who learned quickly and became as loyal a friend as you could want. Tony named him Bingo, and he was a bundle of energy with a natural instinct to chase anything that moved, which made the beach a perfect exercise ground. After chasing and fetching a frisbee multiple times, Bingo was happy to paddle in the shallows while Tony enjoyed his morning swim before they both ran home together.

Soon afterwards, Tony swapped his job at the seal sanctuary for one with the Cornwall Wildlife Trust which paid more and had wider appeal, given its extensive marine conservation programme. He spent the days collecting data on marine wildlife habitats and organising campaigns to create awareness of threats to marine life, and for better protection for marine species and habitats, whether they were tiny, rare, colourful corals found along the coast or giant basking sharks and dolphins.

In his third year with the Trust, he met Iseult, a strong-willed woman with pale grey eyes and a shock of bright red hair, who fancied herself as something of a sorceress, often playing with tarot cards or a ouija board.

'What kind of name is that, anyway?' Tony asked her soon after they had become friends.

'I chose it myself,' she informed him with a shrug. 'It's a name I came across in a book I was reading about the ancient Britons, and I liked it.'

'So, what was your original name, then?'

'Bethany.'

Tony laughed. 'Yeah, I think Iseult is much better. Good choice!'

They grew close, and it wasn't long before she moved in with him, although, at first, they were more companions than lovers, each treasuring their privacy and mostly, but not always, sleeping in their own rooms.

CHAPTER TWENTY-EIGHT

THE GODSON

Tiago was already nearly eleven years old, a strapping youth with a mass of curly black hair, before Roberto and Juliana made their long-promised trip to visit in September 2011. Tony Blair's premiership, the Iraq war and the global financial crisis had all been and gone already; David Cameron had narrowly won the general election the year before and had formed a coalition government with the Liberal Democrats.

Tony drove up to Heathrow to pick Roberto and his family up so they could spend a couple of days in London together to see the sights, although Iseult stayed behind in Cornwall; big cities were not her thing. Roberto was long out of his wheelchair, but still walked with a stick. Apart from that he seemed to have made a full recovery.

'I'm surprised how many Indians and black people there are here,' Juliana remarked, once they had exchanged greetings. 'Even the man who stamped my passport was an Indian. I kind of expected England to be a white country.'

'And thirty to forty years ago, it still was,' Tony replied. 'Blair was the one who really opened the floodgates, so the cities are pretty much all multicultural now. It's good in some ways, but it's happened too fast, so there's been no real chance for proper integration. I'm not even sure that the English are still a majority in London. Or some of the other big cities.'

'Is it safe?'

'Well, put it this way: I wouldn't go around wearing a Rolex, although I wouldn't in Rio either. And keep your mobile phone somewhere safe. A lot of those get snatched. And of course, there are some areas which aren't so safe, but if you stick to the main touristy areas, it's fine. It's different in the countryside, though, especially where I live.'

They booked into the dog-friendly Rose & Crown pub which offered accommodation in Wimbledon village, so Tony and Bingo could go hunting squirrels on the common while his friends went off to see the Tower of London, Buckingham Palace, the Natural History Museum, Big Ben and whatever else took their fancy. On the second afternoon, Tony was joined for lunch at the pub by his old friends James and Sally, who still lived in their same terraced house in the area. They discovered, though, that these days they had little in common.

'So how are you finding life in Cornwall, then?' James asked.

'I love it. I love the quiet, I love the nature, I love the sea, and I love the lack of diversity. It still feels like England.'

'That's a bit racist, isn't it?' Sally interrupted him.

'What do you mean?' Tony asked, taken aback.

'Well, we're a multicultural society now. All cultures are equal, after all.'

'What arrant nonsense! Why do the left always resort to calling people racists just because they have different views? I'm certainly not racist; I've lived happily all over the world, and the issue of race has never come into it. All cultures may be equal in one sense, but they are different too, and frankly I quite like our culture the way it is, or was. Why should I consent to being an ethnic minority in my own country?'

'Steady on, old boy.' James tried to calm things down. 'Things are different now. You need to go with the times.'

'Actually, I don't. I keep reading about the crime levels in places like London now, the stabbings, the terror attacks, how you can't even use your phone in the street without the likelihood of some feral kid stealing it. Around my way, I don't even need to lock the car, I don't need an alarm in the house, and I can go out and leave the windows open without the fear of someone breaking in.'

'Since when did you become so right-wing?' Sally asked.

'Am I right-wing? Is it right-wing not to consent to an alien religion spouting its bile on our streets? Should I just accept our cities being turned into multicultural slums? Why should I accept that we can't deport foreign criminals?'

'But there's always been crime. It's not new; it didn't arrive with immigration,' Sally protested.

'Of course there's always been crime,' Tony conceded. 'But not at the level it is now. Machete-wielding Somalis didn't used to be part and parcel of living in a big city. And what about honour killings, and female genital mutilation, forced marriages and child rape gangs? Why should I be smeared for defending the values of my own people?'

There was a moment's awkward silence while James and Sally glanced at each other, until James acted the peacemaker again. 'Well, I suppose we'll just have to agree to disagree, then. Come on, we've known each other too long to fall out over this. I'll get another round in.'

'You're right,' Tony sighed. 'Although I do feel quite strongly about these issues. The thing is, I don't think it would have come to this if immigration had been managed to levels where the newcomers could be integrated. As it is, there's no chance of integration; the numbers are just too big, so we are getting ghettos.'

'Well, if things do get really rough around here, we'll just have to come and pay you a visit. But let's hope for the best, because it's too late to change back now.'

'It's never too late; things have a habit of going in cycles.' Tony couldn't resist a parting shot. 'But maybe the whole Ponzi scheme that seems to be modern government has to totally collapse first.'

'Now there's a cheerful thought,' Sally said quietly. 'But try not to be so gloomy about it.'

The next morning, Tony, Roberto, Juliana, Tiago and Bingo left early for the six-hour drive to Cornwall. The rain was biblical, but the sky suddenly cleared and the sun made an appearance as they neared Stonehenge on the A303. They stopped to have a look at the prehistoric stone circle and take some photos, even if the entry price put them off from going into the new exhibition centre.

'It's amazing. Shame we can get closer to the stones themselves,' Juliana said.

'That's because idiots kept climbing on them and carving their names on them, so they fenced it off,' Tony explained.

'How old are they? The stones, I mean.'

'Around 4,000 years, apparently. Some of those stones weigh twenty-five tons, and they're not from around here; some are from Wales, I think. Makes you wonder how they got here, maybe by boat, and then up from the coast.'

'What were they for?'

'No one is one hundred percent sure. It might have been religious, or some think it was a kind of calendar, because that big stone there, the one leaning a bit, is aligned with the sunrise on the summer solstice, and if you look the other way it aligns with the winter solstice. Some even think it was a way of communicating between the human and the spirit worlds, or it could have been a burial ground.'

'How do you know all this?'

Tony grinned. 'I cheated. I knew we were coming past Stonehenge, so I looked it up yesterday.'

Soon after leaving the monument, they joined the A30 and finally found themselves on a dual carriageway, bypassing Truro, the capital of Cornwall and the county's only city. Half an hour later they arrived at Porthrepta and Tony's home. He parked up in the driveway, next to a smart caravan he had borrowed from a friend for the two weeks that his Brazilian guests would be staying with him. The door opened, and Iseult came out and was introduced.

'The house is for you,' she said. 'Tony and I will stay in the caravan. Come, I'll show you your rooms; they're all made up.'

'No!' Roberto protested. 'We can't kick you out of the house; the caravan is fine for us!'

'It's non-negotiable,' Iseult told him. 'The house only has two bedrooms, which is perfect for you. The caravan is a bit small for three people, and anyway we love being out in the open. We have keys for the house if we need to come in for the bathroom or whatever, although to be honest we rarely bother locking up anyway.'

They were lucky with the weather and, after walking down to the beach, Tony took off his beach robe, under which he was wearing his swimming trunks. 'Anybody else fancy a dip?'

'Look!' Tiago suddenly pointed. 'What's that?'

What looked like a large dog had appeared in the waves not twenty yards from them and stared, before disappearing under the water again.

Tony laughed. 'It's a grey seal. We get quite a few of them here, especially at this time of the year, when they're starting to breed.'

'Are they dangerous?' Juliana wanted to know.

'Well, they do have a nasty bite on them, but I've only ever heard of one actual attack, and not in this bay. They're curious creatures, though, and they do give you a nudge sometimes, which is a bit scary. But generally, if you give them space and don't get into a staring match with them, which can make them feel threatened, they don't bother you.'

No one else felt like joining Tony, and they watched as he plunged into the water and swam the width of the bay with two seals in tow, while Bingo raced along the waterline barking furiously.

'Isn't it cold?' Roberto asked, when Tony rejoined them on the beach.

'A bit, about seventeen or eighteen degrees centigrade, but that's about as warm as it gets here, so this is the best time of the year. It gets much colder in winter.'

'Hmm. Not sure it's for me, but if the weather stays warm maybe I'll give it a go one day.'

'I've kind of got into that cold water therapy stuff. I think it's really good for you, gets the circulation going and all that.'

'You mean you swim in winter too?' Juliana was astonished.

'Oh yes, most days, except when it's too rough,' Tony said, towelling himself dry before putting his robe back on. 'We get some epic storms down here. But I wear a wetsuit when the temperature starts dipping below fourteen degrees.'

'It's beautiful, though, this coastline with the cliffs, the perfect sand. I never really imagined England like this. I imagined it always grey and raining.'

'Yes, and those cliffs are granite, which means the water we have here is really soft. You'll notice when you take a shower, it takes ages to get the soap off. It tastes better, too.'

Later in the evening, they sat around a fire pit, drinking a decent merlot while Tony grilled ribeye steaks for them all, to go with the potato salad Iseult had prepared earlier. Bingo, having already eaten, slumped onto the grass as close as he could get to the fire without being in danger of combusting.

'Just think, I'll be sixty-five years old next year,' Roberto remarked, looking into the flames. 'Scarcely seems credible, does it?'

'I'm not far behind you, mate,' Tony said. 'A couple more years to go for me. Time to retire, really, although I'm already down to part-time. Tiago, do you swim?'

'Sure.' The youth looked up from the can of Fanta he was nursing.

'Ever tried surfing?'

'No. It looks fun, but isn't it difficult?'

'Not once you get the hang of it. Do you want to try? We could get you some lessons over in Porthmeor; it's only a few miles away. A west-facing beach, decent waves but not a lot of current, so it's safe.'

'I'd love to! What do you think, Papa?'

Roberto nodded. 'Of course, why not?'

'Okay,' Tony said, 'we'll go over tomorrow. I reckon an hour a day for a week should do it. The school will provide the board and a wetsuit.'

Porthmeor was a perfect place for surfers to learn the sport. The beach was wide, with full-time lifeguards on duty, and the waves were steady without being intimidating. The following day they drove over and sorted Tiago out with his lessons, and then Juliana went to visit the nearby Tate Modern gallery, while Roberto and Tony retired to a café overlooking the beach to enjoy a couple of beers in the sunshine while they watched Tiago's efforts. Galleries were something that neither of them had a particular interest in.

On the other days in the week that Tiago was doing his lessons, they wandered the narrow, cobbled streets of nearby St Ives, visiting some of the myriad art shops and a pottery, lunching on pasties and buying souvenirs.

By the fourth day, Tiago was standing up, and by the end of the week he could ride a wave for up to thirty seconds before falling off. He was ecstatic.

'It's fantastic. I'm going to do it every weekend when we get home. I've seen people surfing at Torres!'

'Praia Grande might be best,' said Roberto. 'But we need to check out which beaches have lifeguards.'

The weather remained sublime, which was a relief after a soggy summer, but then increasingly September and October seemed to be the best months. They spent the second week visiting the usual tourist spots – Land's End, St Michael's Mount, the Minack theatre, which especially delighted Juliana, who had never seen anything like it before – and even managed a day trip on the ferry to the Scilly Isles, where they enjoyed a Mediterranean-style lunch of tapas at the Dibble & Grub restaurant on Porthcressa beach.

'We could be on a Greek island,' Tony observed as they drank a local Scillonian white wine, looking out at the sparkling sea. 'Not been here before for some reason, but I'll have to come back and explore a bit more.'

'It's enchanting,' Juliana said. 'I could live here.'

'Might be a bit grim in winter, though.'

All too soon the holiday was over, and Roberto, Juliana and Tiago caught the train for the long, slow journey back to Paddington, and thence to Heathrow to catch their return flight to Brazil. Before they had left, Tony had taken them to a surf shop and bought Tiago a summer 'shorty' wetsuit. 'Not sure how cold the water gets down in

Torres,' he had said to the boy. 'But this should get you started, at least, and maybe it'll remind you of Cornwall.'

'Brilliant, thank you so much. I've loved it down here,' Tiago had told him, giving him a hug. 'I'm glad you're my godfather.'

'I'll miss them,' Tony muttered as he and Iseult watched the train disappear around a bend.

'Yes, they're lovely people. Maybe we can visit them next time?'

'I'd like that. Better start saving up, then.'

Thankfully, now that they had moved into the online age and had mobile telephones with access to WhatsApp, they could keep in regular touch with Roberto and his family through video calls.

'It's amazing that you can call anywhere in the world for free these days,' Tony commented. 'Can you remember what it was like in the old days? And how do they make any money if the calls are free?'

'No idea,' Iseult answered. 'You know I'm not really a techie kind of person. And also, while there are benefits, I'm not convinced all these advances are beneficial, especially social media sites. Inevitable, maybe, but not always beneficial.'

CHAPTER TWENTY-NINE

A Premonition

Time flew. Tony passed his sixty-fifth birthday and retired. The meagre state pension wasn't enough to live on by itself, but over the years he'd made shrewd investments, and he now had a healthy pot of cash and a stash of gold sovereigns to draw on when needed. The latter he bought into when Gordon Brown sold half the country's gold reserves at the bottom of a ten-year bear market; Tony had never had much regard for the Caledonian Cyclops's judgement.

Nevertheless, the days flashed by and he wondered how he'd ever found time to work in the first place. He still swam almost every day, and still did some voluntary work, especially at the food bank, where demand was increasing almost by the day as successive governments seemed to outdo their predecessors in incompetence.

Meanwhile the country was increasingly divided after the Brexit referendum, which the losers refused to accept, and even the governments of Theresa May and Boris Johnson seemed unwilling or unable to implement the verdict, leaving the country with one foot in the European Union and one foot out. Although not officially a member any more, it still followed EU rules, remained a member of the European Court of Human Rights, and effectively gave up sovereignty over Northern Ireland.

'Fucking Theresa May said we seek "no competitive advantage" over the EU,' Tony muttered one night as he and Iseult sat outside. 'Why not? I thought that was the whole point of Brexit? Saggy hag.'

Iseult turned her fierce grey eyes on him and shivered. 'There's evil coming,' she said. 'Dark forces are gathering.' Bingo whimpered in his sleep.

'Huh?' Tony stared back at her. 'Have you been playing with your cards again?'

'Don't mock the tarot, my dear. If you know how to interpret them, they can tell you a lot. There's a reason they've been around for hundreds of years.'

'Okay,' he sighed. 'Out with it, then. Tell me the worst.'

Iseult looked into the flames of their fire pit. 'All I can tell you is general themes. I can't give precise predictions; it's more like a feeling for the way things are going or trending.'

'Go on, then.'

'Okay, the thing is, I've been drawing five cards at a time. You can do different numbers. After each draw, I shuffle the cards before doing it again. And in the last week, I've drawn the same five cards three times, which is unusual to say the least.'

'And? What were the cards, and what do they mean?' Tony took a slug of his beer and again glanced at Iseult, who was still staring into the fire.

'Well, first there was Death, upright, which means a sudden or unexpected upheaval, and a time of change. Or it could also mean a new beginning and spiritual transformation. Second, I got the Hermit reversed, which equates to loneliness and isolation, as if you've lost your way. Third, I drew Justice, also reversed, which means dishonesty, unaccountability and unfairness. Fourth was the Tower, upright, so that's sudden upheaval, broken pride and disaster. And finally, for the fifth, I got the Sun, reversed, and that foretells negativity, depression and sadness.'

'Blimey, that's deep. Not sure I like the sound of all that. What are you suggesting?'

'I'm not suggesting anything, just saying that the omens are not good; we could be in for a rough ride for whatever reason. Maybe we should stock up on essentials, though, just to be on the safe side.'

CHAPTER THIRTY

Lockdown

The Chinese flu, soon renamed coronavirus and then Covid to spare any accusations of anti-Chinese 'racism', officially hit the country early in 2020, and Boris Johnson's government panicked, along with most of the Western world. 'Social distancing' was introduced, then mask wearing, and finally a nationwide lockdown was imposed, closing schools, pubs, restaurants and other businesses. The police were given the power to break up gatherings of more than two people, and everyone was told to stay at home except for going out to exercise once a day or for essential shopping.

There was a massive government campaign to try to force people to take Covid vaccines, while seasonal flu mysteriously disappeared. Even prominent media figures such as Andrew Neil, Piers Morgan, Nick Ferrari and Vanessa Feltz called for sanctions against those who declined to get vaccinated.

'Fuck that,' Tony opined. 'If they've given big pharma immunity against prosecution for these vaccines, then I'm not letting anyone jab me. It all sounds very suspicious.'

'And you can bet some people are making a lot of money out of the scam,' Iseult added.

To top it all, Russia decided to invade Ukraine, announcing that it was to protect ethnic Russians in the east of the country, while clearing Ukraine of 'Nazis'. To many, the invasion hardly came as a surprise after years of NATO expansion to Russia's borders, against all assurances they had given in the past. Johnson was one of the first to rush to Kyiv to promise his undying support for President Volodymyr Zelenskyy, pledging vast amount of British taxpayers' money and weaponry, most of it unaccountable. The war would drag on for years with appalling casualties on both sides.

'Well, looks like your tarot cards weren't so wrong after all,' Tony said. 'Everything has turned to dog shit, and you can bet there are a lot of lonely and depressed people out there right now.'

'This whole lockdown thing is an exercise in control, to see how far they can push people, and the worst thing is, it's working,' Iseult said. 'While the war in Ukraine is just madness. We're living in a clown world.'

Lockdown didn't appear to apply to everyone, though, as thousands of people were allowed to take part in an orgy of riots to protest about the death while being arrested of an African-American junkie with a long criminal record.

Then it all went pear-shaped for Boris Johnson when pictures appeared in the newspapers of him allegedly at death's door with Covid, and then two weeks later new photographs appeared of him hosting a party at number ten Downing Street, and he was driven out of office. The two NHS nurses credited with saving his life, meanwhile, disappeared without a trace.

Conservative party members chose Liz Truss as their next prime minister, ignoring the wishes of their members of parliament, who favoured the Chancellor, Rishi Sunak. Truss, however, lasted just forty-five days, after producing a mini budget which had tax cuts at its core, which her opponents claimed were unfunded, sending the financial markets into turmoil. Sunak was duly installed in her place, with party members being denied a vote this time.

'There's no way a handful of days in power and half a dozen press conferences could have caused the damage they said it did. Everything is being manipulated,' Tony claimed. 'The globalists in the World Economic Forum wanted their man Sunak in power, and now they've got him.'

A year later, interest and mortgage rates were even higher, energy bills were through the roof, inflation was skyrocketing, and illegal immigration to the country was out of control. Lockdown caused massive economic damage, a generation of schoolchildren with myriad mental health issues, and a work-from-home culture, especially amongst civil servants who were reluctant to return to office working.

In the years following, there was also a rash of inexplicable sudden deaths, mostly from blood clots or heart attacks, even amongst otherwise healthy young sportsmen. These deaths were invariably described as 'rare' by the mainstream media, but no real effort was made to link them to the Covid vaccines, especially the ones produced by AstraZeneca, even though the Japanese government decided to discard 13.5 million doses and cancel an order for another 40 million, preferring to stick with the vaccines produced by Pfizer and Moderna instead. Meanwhile the NHS reported than the number of strokes in the over-fifty age group had shot up by fifty-five percent.

Roberto reported from Brazil to say there had been no lockdown in the country, although there was briefly one a year later when deaths started soaring.

'We are managing,' Roberto said. 'We spend a lot of time out at Torres, away from the big cities, and Tiago is still surfing. He's very good at it now.'

'I'm glad to hear it,' Tony told him. 'Maybe we'll try to come out once this is all over, but we'll have to find someone to look after Bingo. What's happening in Amazonia? Do you get any news?'

'Still burning and slashing, as far as I know. I've seen pictures of some parts that look like a desert now.'

'What a mess we're making of this world.'

Sadly, in the end they needed no dogsitter for Bingo. His black fur had been flecked with grey for some time now, and he'd stopped chasing anything that moved, and then one morning he simply didn't wake up. Tony and Iseult were devastated.

'But he wasn't ill, there was nothing wrong with him,' Tony railed, tears streaming down his face as he cradled the small dog's body.

Iseult hugged him from behind. 'It was just his time to go. He was old, and he had a good life.'

'But it seems so unfair. I'm going to miss the bugger.'

Bingo was cremated in a desperately sad ceremony at one of the local veterinary practices, and Tony brought his ashes home and kept the urn in a cupboard.

'When I go, I want my ashes to be mixed with his, okay?'

'Mine too,' Iseult said. 'And then we need someone to commit us all to the sea.'

CHAPTER THIRTY-ONE

Dark Times

The attack by Hamas on an Israeli music festival during a Jewish religious holiday on 7 October 2023 knocked the Ukraine war off the top spot in the foreign news, especially as the Ukrainians were by now beginning to lose ground. More than a thousand Israelis were killed, including women and children, and some 250 Israelis were taken hostage. There were also dozens of reports of rape and sexual assault by the attackers, and the Israeli response was entirely predictable: they decided to flatten Gaza.

As the Israelis pressed ahead with their revenge and desire to rid themselves of Hamas once and for all, pro-Palestinian protests erupted across Europe and the United States. It had become the latest 'thing' to protest about, replacing Just Stop Oil and Black Lives Matter at the top of the protest agenda.

'Why do they always protest here?' Tony mused as he and Iseult sat by their wood-burning stove, the rain hammering at the windows while the wind howled like a banshee. 'Why can't they all just fuck off to the front line if they're so concerned? What's it got to do with us?'

'I just wonder where these people get their money. They always seem to have something to protest about,' Iseult concurred, looking up from her search for flights to Brazil on her laptop. They were planning a trip in the new year. 'Most of them seem to hate us anyway, so I'm not sure why they are here or who let them in.'

'Well, we know the answer to the last question. Blair opened the floodgates, and successive governments have followed the tradition. Fourteen years of Tory rule and they are still piling in, hundreds of thousands a year, and they wonder why there is a shortage of housing, school places and such pressure on the NHS. It's total madness. They can't even stop the illegal immigrants; instead, they send out the lifeboats to give them safe passage.'

Immigration was the other subject that had leapfrogged to the top of the political agenda, with many people angry at the failure of one government after another to stop the daily stream of small boats across the English Channel bringing illegal migrants from across the world. Once in the country, they were given hotel rooms, a phone, three meals a day and pocket money, all at the taxpayer's expense.

'They could have stopped them from day one,' Iseult pointed out. 'The fact that they didn't shows they clearly don't want to.'

'Well, here's the thing,' Tony said, getting up to pour himself a couple of fingers of scotch and offering one to Iseult, who declined. 'I suppose if you were stuck in Africa, you might also consider heading somewhere else – I mean, never mind the climate change bollocks, that continent has always been prone to drought, and it also suffers from poor governance, non-stop ethnic conflicts and endemic corruption, so what is there to stay for?'

'What are you saying, that we should just let them all in?'

'No, not at all; hear me out. What I'm saying is that this phenomenon is not going to go away. It's a massive elephant in the room, and it's certain to get very ugly. Our politicians keep telling us of the wonders of multiculturism, but if we get overwhelmed by hundreds of millions of people from totally different cultures, Europe will not be a happy place to be. The welfare state will inevitably collapse. So, unless radical action is taken, and very soon, we might as well accept that Europe is already culturally and economically finished.'

'There needs to be a popular uprising. That's the only way out of this mess.'

'I think it may already be too late, even for that.'

'I feel dizzy, I can't breathe,' Iseult said suddenly. 'My chest hurts. Tony, help me, I'm scared!'

Tony leapt to her side and felt her wrist. She was sweating and had started to cough, and her heartbeat was far too fast. 'I'm calling an ambulance.'

The nearest accident and emergency hospital was the Royal Cornwall at Treliske near Truro, almost twenty miles away. To their credit, the ambulance reached them in less than an hour, but by this time Iseult was barely conscious.

'What's happening to me?' she croaked.

Tony went with her in the ambulance, but despite the best efforts of the paramedics, Iseult slipped into unconsciousness and was pronounced dead on arrival at the hospital.

Tony was dumbfounded; his brain couldn't compute what had happened. She had seemed so healthy, and now this.

After a post-mortem examination, he was told that she had suffered a pulmonary embolism, whereby a piece of a blood clot from her leg had travelled through the main vein to the right side of her heart. From there, the embolus went to the lungs, where it blocked an artery, cutting the supply of blood to the affected area of the lungs, which in turn decreased the oxygen supply to the brain and the rest of the body with rapid and devastating effect.

Iseult was cremated in a no-frills ceremony, and Tony placed the urn with her ashes alongside Bingo's in the cupboard.

He called Roberto and told him the news, then spent days in some sort of grief-stricken trance, struggling to come to terms with events. He stopped swimming and started drinking and became maudlin. Nothing seemed to matter anymore.

Ten days into his self-imposed solitude, there was a persistent knocking at his door. One of his co-volunteers at the food bank, Ben, a young bearded man in overalls who worked as a carpenter, was standing there, smoking a roll-up. He bent down to the letterbox. 'C'mon, Tony, I know you're in there. Open up, for fuck's sake. I'm not going away until you come out.'

Reluctantly, Tony opened his door. He was unshaven, his clothes were dirty, and he stank of alcohol. 'Go away,' he slurred.

'No way, mate. Look at the state of you. What's happened? You've got to pull yourself together.'

Tony stuck his hands in his pockets, and his shoulders slumped. He started crying again, but, bit by bit, he told Ben the whole sorry story. 'I don't know what to do. I'm lost.'

'People care about you, man. Look at how many you've helped, and they still need your help; we're in desperate times. You'll never be alone, you know? Everyone has been wondering what's happened to you. Come on, first thing is to get you cleaned up. And you need to get off the juice.'

While Tony went to stand under the shower, Ben busied himself with cleaning the cottage, taking out the rubbish, clearing the kitchen of unwashed plates and pans, running the vacuum over the floor and cleaning out the fireplace. The half-empty bottle of whisky was emptied down the sink. The end result wasn't perfect, but it was a big improvement. When Tony came back downstairs wearing clean jeans and shirt, he nodded his approval.

'Thanks, Ben. You're right, I need to snap out of it, but I guess I just got overwhelmed; it's a slippery slope. I still can't get my head around it.'

'No worries. Here, let's go grab a pizza and then go to the food bank. You shouldn't stay alone too much.'

And life went on, as it nearly always does. Tony stayed off the booze for several months and resumed his morning swimming routine, and, when he wasn't helping out at the food bank, he spent many hours just walking, mostly along the coastal path.

He went back to Brazil and spent a month with Roberto and Juliana, and was pleased to see that Tiago was by then an accomplished surfer. The news from the Amazon was not good; deforestation had surged again, mostly under the previous president, Jair Bolsonaro, but he had been replaced by a former president, the left-wing Luiz Inácio Lula da Silva. Roberto hated Lula and had thought never to see him again after his conviction for massive corruption while in power, only for his conviction to have been surprisingly quashed on a technicality a couple of years earlier, paving the way for his return to power in 2023.

'This country is rotten with corruption,' Roberto complained.

'You guys don't know how lucky you are.'

He may have spoken too soon, for the following year Rishi Sunak unexpectedly called a general election to be held in July. The result was a huge majority for Labour under Keir Starmer, which the mainstream media hailed as a 'landslide', even if closer examination of the figures showed that Labour only garnered the votes of marginally over twenty percent of the electorate, with the second lowest turnout since 1918. With Britain's first-past-the-post system, even though the new Reform party got an overall vote share of fourteen percent, they only managed five members of parliament, but came in second place in ninety-eight seats. The Liberal Democrats got fewer votes than Reform, but ended up with seventy-two seats.

Labour was elected on a platform to rebuild the foundations of the country, promising voters an 'ambitious programme driven by belief in the country and its potential'. They promised that all their plans were fully costed and fully funded, and pledged not to raise income tax, national insurance or VAT. Within months the government was embroiled in accusations of sleaze, scandal, cronyism, incompetence and vindictive spitefulness, and their promises were in tatters. Despite constantly trying to blame their Tory predecessors for leaving them a £22 billion 'black hole,' a figure on which the Office for Budget Responsibility (OBR) cast doubt when they said Labour had only inherited £9.5 billion of hidden costs, the government embarked on a massive uncosted and unfunded spending spree.

The stench around the new government worsened still further when Chancellor Rachel Reeves cancelled the winter fuel allowance for ten million pensioners, claiming she didn't want to do it but had been forced to because of the financial 'black hole' left by the previous government. This despite a ten-year-old clip resurfacing of her in the House of Commons saying she supported cutting the winter fuel allowances to some pensioners. Then it emerged that her claims to have been an 'economist' at the Bank of Scotland were false; she had in fact been a fairly junior member of staff in retail banking. Labour spokespeople admitted her CV had been 'embellished'.

'Embellishment. Is that what we call lying now?' Tony asked Ben rhetorically as they packed boxes with tinned and dry foodstuffs.

'They're all the same,' Ben replied. 'They're all at it. The Tories weren't much better, but this lot are really taking the biscuit. No point in voting anymore; all we've got now is the uniparty.'

'What do you suggest? If not through the ballot box, how else are we going to change things?'

'A revolution might help, but it won't happen. As long as people have got their welfare benefits, food, and their big televisions, they'll just keep sitting on their sofas.'

'Well, if they keep up with this net zero nonsense and the blackouts start, maybe that will wake people up?'

Reeves went on to announce a budget which she claimed would raise £40 billion, raising national insurance for employers to fifteen percent, increasing capital gains tax, freezing the level at which inheritance tax was payable until 2030, increasing the minimum wage, increasing the National Health Service budget by more than £22 billion, slapping VAT on private school fees, tripling the free school breakfast budget, increasing the windfall taxes on gas and oil companies, and promising to fund the Ukraine war to a level of £3 billion a year. Inheritance tax was also imposed on farmers whose farms were worth more than £1 million, including machinery.

The markets reacted negatively, the pound sterling fell against the dollar, inflation rose, the economy stagnated, thousands of multimillionaires relocated out of the country, taking their tax money with them, and the livid farmers promised militant action. More than eighty chief executives wrote to Reeves, warning her that increasing their national insurance contributions meant that they faced £7 billion in increased costs, making job losses and higher prices inevitable. It was the biggest tax hike in modern history.

To compound her attacks on businesses of all sizes, and on the farmers, Reeves went on a spending spree, awarding above-inflation pay rises to public workers like NHS staff and teachers, the armed forces and police officers, prison officers and train drivers, and junior doctors, the last being awarded a twenty-two percent pay hike over two years. She also announced massive spending on questionable net zero policies, such as £22 billion for carbon capture and storage, £11 billion on foreign aid, £8.5 billion on GB Energy, and £7.5 billion on a wealth fund. Between July and November, the government's spending on various projects amounted to nearly £70 billion.

'What is this carbon capture and storage?' Tony complained. 'Why don't they just stop cutting down trees and grow some more?'

'Did you know that Coca-Cola and their 500 brands produce 200,000 single-use plastic bottles per *minute,* but now we're told farting cows are the big problem for the environment?' Ben replied.

'Eh? Where did you hear that?'

'Online, and it's true. It's another Bill Gates thing, and they're treating cows with Bovaer to reduce their farting. No one knows if there will be side effects down the line, maybe none, but still, they need to stop messing with the food chain. All this environment stuff is another huge money-making scam. Like replacing a tenth of our agricultural land with solar panels; how's that going to help? Next, they'll be complaining about the numbers of bees and other insects going down, but there's no nectar on a solar panel.'

'You sure it's not just another conspiracy theory? There's a lot of that online.'

'Maybe, but if even a tenth of what's posted online and ignored by the legacy media is true, it's still a huge amount of stuff we're not being told. There are no real journalists any more, just kids on computer screens looking for clickbait.'

'Yeah, you're probably right, and I'd say the online stuff is nearer fifty percent true, if not more. They're all bastards, snouts in the trough and they don't give a fuck about the rest of us.'

Starmer was quickly becoming the most unpopular prime minister in living memory, with approval ratings touching minus fifty, below even those of Tony Blair, which was quite an achievement. But if he thought it couldn't get any worse, Donald

Trump then swept to power in the United States, winning the electoral colleges by a huge margin and with the Republicans also taking control of Congress and the Senate – in an election that mainstream media had claimed was 'neck and neck'.

Starmer had once said that 'humanity and dignity' were two words not understood by Donald Trump, and that 'an endorsement from Donald Trump tells you everything you need to know about what is wrong with Boris Johnson and why he isn't fit to be prime minister'. Starmer's foreign secretary, David Lammy, affectionately known as the 'Tottenham Turnip', had gone further, calling Trump a racist and a KKK Neo-Nazi, and had once said he would be protesting the previous Conservative government's 'capitulation to a tyrant in a toupee', in reference to an invitation to Trump to visit the United Kingdom during his earlier presidency.

Part of Starmer's answer seemed to be to embark on an unprecedented number of foreign trips. Within four months he had clocked up sixteen overseas visits, more than any predecessor, and he came under criticism for not paying more attention to the problems at home. It also earned him another sobriquet, of 'Never Here Keir', to add to 'Two Tier Keir' and 'Free Gear Keir'.

'Okay, so now he's TTFGNHK,' Tony said, with a laugh. 'Sounds like LGBTQ+ or whatever it is.'

'Except it's not really funny,' Ben retorted, picking up another tin of baked beans and some breakfast cereal to pack.

'Gotta hit rock bottom and have total collapse before we can start rebuilding, and this lot are sure taking us there at an alarming rate.'

'I'm more worried about us and the Yanks throwing long-range missiles at Ivan. What if they go full nuclear and flatten us?'

'Well, I've got my iodine tablets. Not that they will help much, but you know what? I don't really give a fuck any more if there is a nuclear war.'

CHAPTER THIRTY-TWO

A Bigger Problem

Tony spent a quiet Christmas, part of the problem being that he felt tired all of the time; his energy levels seemed to have dropped off alarmingly. He also noticed that the whites of his eyes had yellowed, and he often suffered back or stomach pains, which seemed worse when he lay down. Finally, after suffering a prolonged bout of diarrhoea, he dragged himself off to his local doctor, something he was always reluctant to do, believing that the less contact you had with doctors, the less chance they could find something wrong with you.

'Have you been losing weight?' the doctor, a German called Holtzman, asked.

'I guess. A bit, anyway, but then I rarely feel hungry these days,' Tony admitted.

'And your skin is a bit yellow, it's not just the eyes, which might suggest jaundice. We need to organise a scan for you to get a better idea.'

The scan was carried out at the Royal Cornwall, the same hospital where Iseult had been taken the day she had died, which brought back bad memories. Two days later Tony got a call from Dr Holtzman asking if he could come into his surgery.

'It's not great news, I'm afraid,' the doctor told Tony without further ado. 'It seems you have pancreatic cancer.'

'What does that mean? Is it bad? I don't even know what the pancreas is.'

Dr Holtzman removed his spectacles and looked at Tony with a frown. 'The pancreas is an organ in the top part of the tummy, which helps digest food and makes hormones such as insulin.'

'And what are my options?' Tony felt remarkably calm in the circumstances, almost as if he were discussing the weather rather than a possibly fatal disease.

'We'll need to do some more tests, to determine how far advanced it is. If it's not too advanced, we can try surgery to stop the pancreas getting blocked. If it's advanced, then we would be looking at palliative care to help you to live longer.'

'And what are the survival chances like? You can be honest with me.'

'I will be. Pancreatic cancer is one of the worst. It's known as the "silent cancer" because the signs of the disease are fairly common and often go unnoticed.'

'And?'

'Well, it has a very low survival rate. Overall, less than ten percent of people with it survive. It's common for death to come within three months. I'm sorry.'

Tony sat with his head in his hands for some moments. 'Don't be sorry, doctor; it's not your fault.' He looked up. 'And you know, if it's bad, then the sooner I go, the better. I've had a good innings.'

'We can try radiation therapy or chemotherapy if surgery isn't possible.'

'I'll think about it. Let's get those tests done first.'

Additional tests were conducted over the next couple of weeks, and the prognosis was not good. The cancer was in an advanced stage, ruling out surgery. The only alternative was palliative care.

'Not sure what to do,' Tony confided to his friend Ben as they spent an evening at their regular pizza place on the day Trump was inaugurated as the forty-seventh president of the United States. 'I'm thinking of just ending it all, now that parliament has passed its assisted dying act.'

'I wouldn't trust our lot to get even that right,' Ben said, helping himself to a slice of his favourite pizza Napoli, a tomato base with olives and anchovies. 'Anyway, I doubt it will be operational for a couple of years yet; still a lot of committee stages to go through.'

'They did seem to rush it through, though. If I remember

correctly, parliament spent about 700 hours debating whether to ban the killing of foxes, but only six hours to agree on the killing of humans.'

'Assisted suicide. Call it what it is. But if you really feel like that, there's always that place in Switzerland,' Ben suggested through a mouthful. 'Not that I think you should do that.'

'Dignitas. Yes, I've heard of it. Well, it's an option, I suppose, although I was quite looking forward to seeing how Trump will drain the swamp. Wouldn't want to miss that,' Tony replied, pushing his half-eaten plate away. 'And once he's finished, maybe he can help drain ours.'

After studying their website, however, a couple of days later Tony paid 220 Swiss francs to become a member of Dignitas, and made an appointment to visit their offices. The week after, he found himself in a discreet house in the upmarket commuter village of Forch, a few miles outside Zürich, where a sign in reception declared, *"To live with dignity, to die with dignity".* He supposed it was their motto. The doctor in front of him was a slim, dapper man with silver hair cut very short, Tony guessed around fifty years old.

Once Tony had outlined his situation, the doctor, Wolfgang Steinbeck, steepled his fingers and pursed his lips. 'Well, you would certainly qualify if you want to go down the road of assisted dying, but it's something you should think very carefully about before committing yourself.'

'I have thought about it a lot already, and I think I would like to proceed. But out of interest, how does all of this align with your Hippocratic oath?'

Dr Steinbeck shrugged. 'Hippocrates was more than 2,000 years ago. Times have changed. And you realise you have to administer the drug yourself? We can't do it for you, otherwise it raises all kinds of moral and ethical issues; in effect that would be euthanasia.'

'Yes, I understand all of that. I suppose it's better than jumping in front of a train. But it seems to be a slippery slope.'

'Perhaps you are right. Time will tell.'

They agreed an appointment for a month later, and Tony paid precisely 9,000 Swiss francs in advance, which was equivalent to just over £8,000. It was also agreed he could be accompanied by a friend.

Back in England, he called Roberto and told him what he was planning, and that he wanted to leave his cottage to Tiago, as he had no other family. His friend was aghast but supportive, and promised to fly over to be with him when the day came.

CHAPTER THIRTY-THREE

An Awakening

Roberto and Tony flew together to Zürich, and told the exorbitant airport taxi driver where they needed to go in the village of Pfäffikon.

'Ah, so you go to the Blue House, then?'

'The what?'

'The Blue House. That's what we call it.'

'Why is that?'

'Because it is blue. You will see.'

Sure enough, after driving a dozen or so miles southeast of Zürich, along the shores of the Zürichsee, they pulled up in front of a house with blue metallic cladding on some sort of semi-industrial estate. Dr Steinbeck was waiting inside to show Tony to his room, and recommended a nearby guest house where Roberto could stay the night. Before Roberto left, the two of them went for a walk in the garden, and sat by the small stream which ran through it.

'Are you sure about this?' Roberto asked softly.

'I think so.'

'That means you're not. Are you in a lot of pain?'

'Some days are worse than others. But the thought of being on borrowed time is always hanging over me. I just feel I should exit stage left while my mind is clear, before things deteriorate further.'

'We'll miss you.'

After Roberto had departed for the night, Tony returned to his room, where a lovely young nurse with a name tag that identified her as *A Nagy* served him his nominated last dinner: steak tartare with a rocket side salad, followed by strawberries and cream, washed down with a glass of local pinot noir. At his request, the nurse sat with him as he ate and regaled her with stories of his life.

Later, he had trouble falling asleep, and found himself thinking of all of the big events in his varied life, what had made him happy and what had made him sad. Water Flower Garden remained the high point, the time when he thought he had finally found real meaning in his life but which had then been snatched from his grasp. Much of the rest of the time he seemed to have been chasing shadows, constantly searching for, but never quite finding, the elusive key to unlock the purpose of it all. In the end he decided there was no real meaning, and he fell to thinking about the women in his life, those he had genuinely loved, before at last he fell into a deep and untroubled sleep.

He was already awake when there was a light tap on his door the following morning. 'Come in!' he called, and he was delighted to see the same nurse enter with his breakfast tray. Her eyes were a stunning, very pale blue. 'Alex, good morning!'

'How are you feeling today?' she asked.

'Pretty good, actually. I might take a walk when my friend arrives, before, you know, Dr Steinbeck is due.'

'Of course.' Alex sat on the bed while she poured him a coffee. 'You don't mind if I sit here?'

'Mind? No, no, absolutely not. On the contrary, I welcome the company.'

She took his hand and gave it a squeeze. 'I always feel sad saying goodbye to patients.'

Tony put his cup down on the side table, and then gasped in surprise as Alex slipped her hand under the duvet and fondled him. He was immediately hard, and, moments later, experienced an excruciating pleasure as he ejaculated.

'Oh my, I wasn't expecting that!' he breathed out heavily, grinning. 'I'd almost forgotten what it was like. Is it all part of the service?'

'It'll be our little secret,' she told him as she took a tissue and cleaned him. 'And no, I've never done something like that before. But there's something about you, I loved your stories last night, and

I just wanted to give you some happiness before you leave us.'

'You've certainly done that! I only wish I could thank you properly.'

'No need; as I said, it's our little secret. I don't know what came over me.'

She left with his breakfast tray soon afterwards, and Roberto arrived as Tony came out of the shower, his face still flushed. 'You're looking chipper this morning, my friend!'

'Yes, something's happened. I'll explain later, but suddenly I feel, well, full of life!'

'Full of life? But...'

Before he could say more, there was another knock on the door, and Dr Steinbeck came into the room with Alex, who gave Tony a shy smile.

'Mr Tony,' the doctor addressed him. 'Did you have a pleasant evening?'

'Very pleasant, in the circumstances, thank you. And a lovely breakfast.'

'Good, good, I am happy to hear that. I just wanted to talk you through the procedure once more, so you are clear.'

'Of course.'

'First, we will give you an anti-emetic, which prevents nausea and vomiting. Afterwards we will ask you to take a drink with sodium pentobarbital; it is flavoured, so it's not an unpleasant taste. You will fall asleep within two to five minutes before slipping into a deep coma. After some time, the sodium pentobarbital will paralyse the respiratory centre, which leads to death, but it is utterly painless.' He looked at his watch. 'We will return in one and a half hours. Until then you are free to walk in the garden and take some fresh air, or whatever you like.'

'Thank you. But I've changed my mind, doctor.'

'I beg your pardon?' Dr Steinbeck looked startled.

'I said I've changed my mind. I'm not going through with it. This morning, I had a revelation.' Tony threw a quick glance at Alex, who blushed. Roberto was grinning. 'I'll just pack my bag and take my leave, if that's all right with you.'

'Well, this has never happened before! I don't understand, what has changed your mind? And you know we can't offer a refund.'

'You can keep the money,' Tony told him, standing up and offering his hand. 'I've just had second thoughts, that's all.'

Dr Steinbeck shook his hand cautiously. 'Well, of course, it's your decision, but it is a little surprising.'

'You sound disappointed.'

'Oh, no, no, not at all, but it is highly unusual. As I said, it has never happened before.'

While they sat in the airport lounge waiting for their flight back to England, after buying an extra ticket for Tony at the last minute, Tony told Roberto what had happened. 'You know, in that moment, I suddenly realised I didn't want to die, that life can still be full of wonderful surprises. It was like an epiphany; that girl saved my life! I also understood in a flash that I've been chasing the idea of happiness all of my life, chasing shadows, when all the time it's been right inside; it's appreciating the moment. It's about giving and not expecting anything back, and friends, like yourself: all the little good things which add up and are paradise in themselves. I suddenly feel incredibly lucky.'

Roberto doubled over laughing, then slapped Tony on the back. 'Well, senhor, I for one am delighted. Juliana and Tiago will be as well. You have made the right decision, and we will have many more good times together; be sure of that. You know, there was an Austrian psychoanalyst called Bruno something, a Holocaust survivor, who said something like that if we want to live in true consciousness, then our greatest need and most difficult achievement is to find meaning in our lives. Now you have done it!'

'That's interesting; I should read him. Do you know his other name?'

'Bertlesman, maybe? Or Bettelsman, perhaps; no, Bettelheim, that's it!' They stood as their flight was called and made their way towards the gate.

And Roberto was right about them sharing many more good

times, as Tony defied all the odds and lived through two more Christmases, both of which they spent together. He was always in some pain, but it was bearable, and he was even able to continue with his regular swimming as long as there was no north wind blowing and the sea wasn't too choppy.

In the end, it wasn't even the cancer that did for him. During one of his morning swims in early March, when the sea was at its coldest, Tony suffered a cardiac arrest. He had taken to wearing a buoyant tow float around his waist, which stopped him sinking. A fellow wild swimmer heard his cry of pain and rushed to drag him to the beach and began giving him CPR, frantically pushing down on his chest and releasing the pressure every couple of seconds, while a dog walker called the coastguard. The local lifeboat and air-sea rescue helicopter arrived almost simultaneously, a little over half an hour later, but it was already too late. Tony was cremated, according to his wishes, and his ashes mixed with those of Bingo and Iseult.

Two weeks later, Ben, along with other former colleagues from the food bank and old friends from the Cornwall Wildlife Trust and seal sanctuary, joined Roberto, Juliana and Tiago at the far end of Porthrepta beach to scatter the remains in the water, and later to give Tony a proper send-off at a local hostelry.

'Look!' Tiago cried, pointing out to sea as the urn emptied. As if by magic they watched as a pod of dolphins crossed the bay not thirty yards away, leaping and diving, the sun glinting silver off their backs as they rose from the water. 'They've come to say goodbye too!'

Follow the author on FB, LinkedIn or nfparsons@yahoo.co.uk

Printed in Great Britain
by Amazon